George Robert Gray

Catalogue of the Birds of the Tropical Islands of the Pacific Ocean, in the Collection of the British Museum

Anatiposi

George Robert Gray

Catalogue of the Birds of the Tropical Islands of the Pacific Ocean, in the Collection of the British Museum

Reprint of the original.

1st Edition 2023　|　ISBN: 978-3-38230-838-4

Anatiposi Verlag is an imprint of Outlook Verlagsgesellschaft mbH.

Verlag (Publisher): Outlook Verlag GmbH, Zeilweg 44, 60439 Frankfurt, Deutschland
Vertretungsberechtigt (Authorized to represent): E. Roepke, Zeilweg 44, 60439 Frankfurt, Deutschland
Druck (Print): Books on Demand GmbH, In de Tarpen 42, 22848 Norderstedt, Deutschland

CATALOGUE

OF THE

BIRDS

OF THE

TROPICAL ISLANDS OF THE PACIFIC OCEAN,

IN THE COLLECTION OF THE

BRITISH MUSEUM.

BY

GEORGE ROBERT GRAY, F.L.S., F.Z.S., ETC.

LONDON:

PRINTED BY ORDER OF THE TRUSTEES.

1859.

PREFACE.

THE object of the present List has been to give a complete Catalogue of the species of Birds (under their respective specific names, with their synonyms) as found on the numerous Islands of the Pacific Ocean, which are situated within the tropic between the longitudes of 134° E. and 130° W.

The space thus circumscribed embraces the groups of the Pelew, Ladrone, Caroline, Marshall's, Gilbert's, and Sandwich Islands, and various other scattered islands on the north of the Equator. It also includes those of the Admiralty, New Britain, New Ireland, Solomon, and Queen Charlotte's Islands, New Hebrides, New Caledonia, Loyalty, Feejee, Samoan, Tonga, Cook's, Austral, Society, Low, and Marquesas Islands, as well as the other outlying islands on the south of the Equator.

Latham in his 'General Synopsis' was the first author who described the different species of Birds of the numerous tropical islands, specimens of which were obtained, or were represented in the many drawings made by Sydney Parkinson, the Forsters, and Ellis, during the three Voyages undertaken by the great circumnavigator Cook. To these are added, those recorded in the zoological portions of the different foreign Voyages of discovery, as well as others which have been procured by the more modern collectors.

The species contained in the Museum Collection, from one or other of the localities noticed, are exemplified by the letters B.M. It may further be observed, that specimens of some of the other species, noted in the Catalogue, may also be seen in the Museum Collection as from other localities.

JOHN EDWARD GRAY.

October 1, 1859.

CATALOGUE

BIRDS

OF THE

TROPICAL ISLANDS OF THE PACIFIC OCEAN.

AVES.

FALCONIDÆ.

PANDION HALIAËTUS (?).

Falco haliaëtus, Forst. Descr.* &c. p. 257.

Isle of Pines (Island of Spruce Trees); Tonga Islands (Tonga-tabu or Tonga Island).

PANDION (POLIOAËTUS) SOLITARIUS.

Buteo solitarius, Peale, U. S. Expl. Exped. p. 62.
Pandion (Polioaëtus) solitarius, Cass. U. S. Expl. Exped. (1858) p. 97. pl. 4.

Sandwich Islands or Isle de la Mesa (Hawaii or Owhyhee).

CUNCUMA LEUCOGASTER.

Falco leucogaster, Gmel. S. N. i. p. 257.
Falco blagrus, Daud. Tr. d'Orn. ii. p. 70?
Haliaëtus leucogaster, Gould, Syn. of B. Austr. iii. p.   .
Haliaëtus sphenurus, Gould, Syn. of B. Austr. iii. p.   .
Cuncuma leucogaster, G. R. Gray.
Haliaëtus (Pontoaëtus) leucogaster, Kaup.
Ichthyiaëtus leucogaster, Gould, B. of Austr. i. pl. 3.

New Ireland (Port Praslin).

* Descr. Anim., edit. by Lichtenstein, 1844.

B

HALIASTUR LEUCOSTERNUS, var.

Haliastur leucosternus, G. R. Gray, List of B. B.M. i. p. 13.
Falco ponticerianus, Shaw, Nat. Misc. pl. 389.
Haliaëtus leucosternus, Gould, Proc. Z. S. 1837, p. 138 ; B. of
Austr. i. pl. 4.
Haliaëtus (Ictinoaëtus) leucosternus, Kaup.
New Ireland (Carteret Harbour).

HALIASTUR SPHENURUS.

Milvus sphenurus, Vieill. N. Dict. Hist. Nat. xx. p. 564.
Haliaëtus canorus, Vig. & Horsf. Linn. Trans. xv. p. 187.
Haliastur? *sphenurus*, Gould, B. of Austr. i. pl. 5.
New Caledonia (Port S. Vincent).

ACCIPITER APPROXIMANS.

Astur approximans, Vig. & Horsf. Linn. Trans. xv. p. 181 ; Gould,
B. of Austr. i. pl. 17.
New Caledonia (Island of Nu).

ACCIPITER HAPLOCHROUS.

Accipiter haplochrous, Sclater, Ibis, 1859, p. 275. pl. 8.
New Caledonia (Island of Nu).

ACCIPITER RUFITORQUES.   B.M.

Astur rufitorques, Peale, U.S. Expl. Exped. p. 68.
Accipiter rufitorques, Pucher. Voy. au Pôle Sud, i. p. 49.
Voy. au Pôle Sud, Ois. t. 2. f. 2.
U. S. Expl. Exped. pl. 2. f. 1, 2.
' Manu levu ' of the natives.
Feejee or Fiji or Fedjee or Fidjee or Fidschi Islands, or Iles Viti
(Ovolau).

CIRCUS ASSIMILIS.

Circus assimilis, Jard. & Selby, Ill. of Orn. pl. 51 ; Cass. U. S.
Expl. Exped. (1858) p. 101.
Circus approximans, Peale, U. S. Expl. Exped. p. 64.
Feejee Islands (Venua or Vanua Levu or Tacanova or. Paoo or
Kautaou).

STRIGIDÆ.

ATHENE FORSTERII.

Strix bakkamuna?, Forst. Descr. &c. pp. 157, 256.
Athene Forsteni (Forsteri), Pr. B. Consp. Av. i. p. 42.
Strix Forsteri, (Bp.) Hartl. Wiegm. Arch. für Naturg. 1852,
p. 130.
Tonga Islands (Tongatabu or Amsterdam Island, Annamooka or
Anamocka or Namouka or Rotterdam Island, Tupai) ; New He-
brides or New Cyclades or Archip. de Quiros (Tanna).

ATHENE TÆNIATA.

Athene tæniata, Homb. & Jacq. Voy. au Pôle Sud, i. p. 50. t. 3. f. 1.
Athene Jacquinoti, Pr. B. Consp. Av. i. p. 29.

Solomon or Salomon Islands or New Georgia (St. George).

ATHENE VARIEGATA.

Noctua variegata, Quoy & Gaim. Voy. de l'Astrol. i. p. 166. t. 1. f. 2.
Athene variegata, G. R. Gray, Gen. of B. i. p. 35.

New Ireland (Carteret Harbour).

OTUS BRACHYOTUS, var.

Otus brachyotus, (Wils.) Peale, U. S. Expl. Exped. p. 75.
Brachyotus galapagoensis, (Gould) Cass. U. S. Expl. Exped. (1858) p. 107.
Strix sandvicensis, Bloxh. Byron's Voy. p. 250.
' Puaho ' or ' Pouéhou ' of the natives of the Sandwich Islands.
' Monmou ' of the natives of the Ladrone Islands.

Sandwich Islands ; Ladrone or Marian or Marianne Islands.

STRIX DELICATULA.   B.M.

Strix delicatula, (Gould)? G. R. Gray, List of Accip. 1848, p. 110;
Cass. U. S. Expl. Exped. (1858) p. 105.
Strix lulu, Peale, U. S. Expl. Exped. p. 74.
' Lulu' of the natives of the Samoan Islands.

Samoan or Navigators' Islands, or Hamoa ; Feejee Islands (Ovolau) ; Tonga Islands (Tongatabu) ?

HIRUNDINIDÆ.

COLLOCALIA CINEREA.

Ash-bellied Swallow, Lath. Gen. Syn. ii. p. 573.
Hirundo peruviana, Forst. Descr. &c. p. 240 ; G. Forst. Icon. ined. 168*.
Hirundo cinerea, pt., Gmel. S. N. i. p. 1026.
Macropteryx leucophæus, Peale, U. S. Expl. Exped. p. 178.
Collocalia cinerea, (Gm.) Cass. U. S. Expl. Exped. (1858) p.183. pl. 12. f. 4.
Herse peruviana, Hartl. Wiegm. Arch. für Naturg. 1852, p. 130.
Cypselus leucophaea, Pr. B. Rivista Contemp. 1857, p. .
' Hopea ' of the natives of the Society Islands.

Society Islands or Iles Taiti or K. George's Isles (Otaheite or Tahiti) ; Friendly Islands (Apye or Api or Hapai or Hapace? or Haabai? or Galvez Islands).

COLLOCALIA SPODIOPYGIA.   B.M.

Macropteryx spodiopygia, Peale, U. S. Expl. Exped. i. p. 176.

* Collection of Drawings made during Cook's Second Voyage in the years 1772-75, in the Banksian Collection of the British Museum.

Collocalia spodiopygia, Cass. U. S. Expl. Exped. (1858) p. 184. pl. 12. f. 3.

Hirundo francica, (Gmel.) ? Cass.

Cypselus spodiopygia, Pr. B. Rivista Contemp. 1857, p. .

Ellis's Icon. ined. 96 *.

Samoan or Navigators' Islands (Oyolava or Ohatooa or Opolu or Oatooah or Upolu); Feejee Islands (Ovolau).

COLLOCALIA FUCIPHAGA (?).

Collocalia (Salangana) fuciphaga, (Thunb.) Pr. B. Compt. Rend. 1855, p. 1112.

' Kopeka ' of the natives of the Marquesas Islands.

Marquesas or Marquis of Mendoza's or Washington's Islands, or Iles de Mendana, or Iles Nouka-Hiva, or Ingraham Islands ; Caroline Islands or New Philippines (Oualan or Ualan or Ulalan) ; Society Islands (Otaheite) ?

COLLOCALIA TROGLODYTES (?).

Collocalia troglodytes, (G. R. Gray) Pr. B. Compt. Rend. 1855, p. 977.

New Caledonia.

COLLOCALIA VANIKORENSIS.

Hirundo vanikorensis, Quoy & Gaim. Voy. de l'Astrol. i. p. 206. t. 12. f. 3.

Atticora? vanikorensis, G. R. Gray, Gen. of B. i. p. 58.

Collocalia fuciphaga, pt.?, Pr. B. Rivista Contemp. 1857, p. .

Island of Vanikoro or Manicolo, or Aldersey or Pitt's Island.

HIRUNDO TAHITICA.

Otaheite Swallow, Lath. Gen. Syn. ii. p. 563. pl. (title-page of vol.).

Hirundo pyrrholaema, Forst. Descr. &c. p. 241 ; G. Forst. Icon. ined. 167.

Hirundo tahitica, Gmel. S. N. i. p. 1016.

Herse tahitica, Hartl. Wiegm. Arch. für Naturg. 1852, p. 130.

Cecropsis tahitensis, Boie.

Hirundo taitensis, Less. Voy. Coqu. i. p. 648.

Petrochelidon tahitica, Pr. B. Rivista Contemp. 1857, p. .

' Opea ' or ' Hopéä ' of the natives.

Society Islands (Otaheite).

? HIRUNDO SUBFUSCA.   B.M.

Hirundo subfusca, Gould, Proc. Z. S. 1856, p. 137.

Phedina subfusca, Pr. B. Rivista Contemp. 1857, p. .

Hirundo tahitica?, G. R. Gray.

Feejee Islands (Moala or Mouala).

* A series of Zoological Drawings made during Cook's Third Voyage in the years 1776–79, in the Banksian Collection of the British Museum.

ALCEDINIDÆ.

HALCYON ALBICILLA.

Alcedo albicilla, Cuv. Dumont, Dict. des Sci. xxix. p. 273.
Dacelo albicilla, Less. Tr. d'Orn. p. 247.
Halcyon albicilla, G. R. Gray, Gen. of B. i. p. 79.
Todiramphus albicilla, Pr. B. L'Ateneo Ital. 1854, p. .

Ladrone or Marian Islands ; New Ireland (Port Praslin).

HALCYON CINNAMOMINA.   B.M.

Halcyon cinnamominus, Sw. Zool. Illustr. pl. 67.
Dacelo ruficeps, Cuv. Less. Tr. d'Orn. i. p. 247.
Todiramphus Reichenbachii, Hartl. Wiegm. Arch. für Naturg.
1852, p. 131 ?
Todiramphus cinnamominus, Cass. Expl. Exped. (1858) p. 220.
Todiramphus ruficeps, Pr. B. L'Ateneo Ital. 1854, p. .
' Kiou kiou ' of the natives of New Ireland.

Ladrone or Marian Islands ; New Caledonia ; New Hebrides ;
Solomon Islands ; New Ireland (Port Praslin).

HALCYON VITIENSIS.   B.M.

Halcyon superciliosa, G. R. Gray, List of Fissir. B.M. p. 56.
Alcedo collaris, var. I., Forst. Descr. &c. p. 163.
Dacelo vitiensis, Peale, U. S. Expl. Exped. p. 156.
Todiramphus vitiensis, Hartl. Wiegm. Arch. für Naturg. 1852,
p. 130 ; Cass. U. S. Expl. Exped. (1858) pp. 195, 209. pl. 16.
Todiramphus superciliosus?, Hartl. Wiegm. Arch. für Naturg.
1852, p. 130.

Tonga Islands (Tongatabu) ; Feejee Islands (Viti Levu or Am-
bow or Ambau, Ovolau, Venua Levu).

HALCYON ——— ?

Alcedo collaris, var. II., Forst. Descr. &c. p. 163.
Todiramphus, sp.?, Hartl. Wiegm. Arch. für Naturg. 1852, p.131.

Marquesas Islands (Insula S^{tæ} Christinæ or Christmia or St.
Christiana or Waitahoo or Tabouata or Ohitahoo ?).

HALCYON CORONATA.   B.M.

Dacelo coronata, Peale, U. S. Expl. Exped. p. 160.
Todiramphus tuta, Cass. U. S. Expl. Exped. 1858, pp. 192, 206.
pl. 15. f. 1.
Todiramphus coronatus, Hartl. Wiegm. Arch. für Naturg. 1852,
p. 130.
Todiramphus sacer, pt., Cass. Cat. of Halcyon. p. .
' Nethug' of the natives of New Hebrides.

Samoan or Navigators' Islands (Tutuila or Tootooillah or Maouna) ;
? New Hebrides (Erromango or Koromango, Aneiteum or Annatom
or Annotam or Anattom).

HALCYON SANCTA.   B.M.

Halcyon sanctus, Vig. & Horsf. Linn. Trans. xv. p. 206.
Alcedo vagans, Less. Voy. de la Coqu. Zool. i. p. 696.
Todiramphus sanctus, Pr. B. L'Ateneo Ital. 1854, p.   .

Loyalty Islands ; New Caledonia (Island of Nu, Port de France) ;
New Hebrides ; Solomon Islands.

HALCYON (TODIRAMPHUS) PLATYROSTRIS.   B.M.

Todiramphus recurvirostris, Lafr. Rev. Zool. 1842, p. 134.
Halcyon platyrostris, Gould, Proc. Z. S. 1842, p. 72.
Dacelo minima, Peale, U. S. Expl. Exped. p. 159. pl. 17.
Todiramphus platyrostris, Pr. B. L'Ateneo Ital. 1854, p.   .

Samoan or Navigators' Islands (Upolu).

HALCYON (TODIRAMPHUS) VENERATA.   B.M.

Todiramphus sacer, Less. Voy. de la Coqu. i. p. 686 ; Mém. Soc.
Hist. Nat. Paris, iii. p. 421. t. 11.
Dacelo albifrons, Peale's MSS. ?
Todiramphus tuta, pt., Cass. Expl. Exped. 1858, p. 208. pl. 15. f. 2.
Venerated Kingsfisher, Lath. Gen. Syn. i. p. 623 *.
Alcedo venerata, Gmel. S. N. i. p. 453 ; Pelzelu, Sitzungs. Acad.
Vienna, 1856, xx. p. 503.
Halcyon venerata, G. R. Gray, Gen. of B. i. p. 79.
Todiramphus veneratus, Pr. Br. L'Ateneo Ital. 1854, p.   .
Ellis's Icon. ined. 22 (?), 23.

Friendly Islands (Apye) ; Samoan or Navigators' Islands (Tutuila).

HALCYON (TODIRAMPHUS) SACRA.   B.M.

Sacred Kingsfisher, Lath. Gen. Syn. i. p. 621 (nearly adult ?).
Alcedo sacra, Gmel. S. N. i. p. 453.
Alcedo cyanea, Forst. Descr. &c. p. 156.
Halcyon sacra, G. R. Gray, Gen. of B. i. p. 79.
Todiramphus tuta, pt., Cass. U. S. Expl. Exped. 1858, p. 208.
pl. 15. f. 3.
Todiramphus sacer, Hartl. Wiegm. Arch. für Naturg. 1852, p. 130.
Sacred Kingsfisher, var. A, Lath. Gen. Syn. i. p. 621 (adult).
Alcedo sacra, var. β, Gmel.
Respected Kingsfisher, Lath. Gen. Syn. i. p. 624 (young).
Alcedo tuta, Gmel. S. N. i. p. 453.
Halcyon tuta, G. R. Gray, Gen. of B. i. p. 79.
Alcedo collaris, Forst. Descr. &c. p. 162 ; G. Forst. Icon. ined. 58.
Todiramphus divinus, Less. Voy. de la Coqu. i. p. 687 ; Mém.
Soc. H. N. Paris, iii. t. 12.
Dacelo nullitorquis, Peale, U. S. Expl. Exped. p. 155. pl. 18. f. 1.
Todiramphus nullitorques, Hartl. Wiegm. Arch. für Naturg. 1852,
p. 130.

'Eròoro' or 'O-tataré' or 'Kooto-o-oo' of the natives.

Society Islands (Tahiti, Ulietea or Raïetea, Borabora or Bolabola).

* Mus. Vienna.

? HALCYON (TODIRAMPHUS) —— ?

Sacred Kingsfisher, var. B, Lath. Gen. Syn. i. p. 622. pl. 27.
Alcedo sacra, var. γ, Gmel. S. N. i. p. 453.

Society Islands (Ulietea).

HALCYON (CYANALCYON) LEUCOPYGIA.   B.M.

Cyanalcyon leucopygius, Verr. Rev. et Mag. de Zool. 1858, p. .

Top of head, scapulars, and wings black, each feather margined
with deep indigo-blue ; base of lower mandible and ear-coverts deep
black ; tail blue-black ; under wing-coverts and the entire under
surface white ; tail-coverts indigo-blue ; under tail-coverts and side
of tail castaneous, tinged with pale purple ; thighs black ; bill and
feet black.
Length 7″; wings 3″ 3‴.
Solomon Islands.

HALCYON (ACTINOIDES?) JACQUINOTI.

Alcedo diophthalmo-rufo-ventro, Hombr. & Jacq. Ann. des Sci.
Nat. n. s. xvi. p. 315.
Actenoides Hombroni, (Pr. B.) Hartl. Wiegm. Arch. für Naturg.
1852, p. 130.
Halcyon MacLeayii, (Jard. & Selby) ? Cass. Cat. of Halcyon. p. .

Tonga Islands (Vavao or Howe's Island).

Note.—Quoy and Gaimard record a species of "*Martin Chas-
seur*" as found in the Island of Vanikoro (Voy. de l'Astrol. Zool. i.
p. 162), but they have not given any description of it.

Latham has recorded the two following birds as from the South
Seas (?), which must belong to this genus, viz. :—

Black-capped Kingsfisher, var. B, Lath. Gen. Syn. i. p. 626.
Ferruginous-bellied Kingsfisher, Lath. Hist. of B. iv. p. 34.

ALCEDO —— ?

Alcedo ispida, var. *Moluccana*, Less. & Garn. Voy. de la Coqu.
Zool. i. pp. 343, 694.

New Ireland (Port Praslin).

PROMEROPIDÆ.

DREPANIS PACIFICA.

Great Hook-billed Creeper, Lath. Gen. Syn. i. p. 703.
Certhia pacifica, Gmel. S. N. i. p. 470 ; Ellis's Icon. ined. 27 ;
Vieill. Ois. dor. t. 63 ; Levaill. Hist. de la Guêp. t. 19.
Vestiaria hoho, Less.

Melitreptus pacificus, Vieill. Encyc. Méth. p. 602.
Drepanis pacifica, Temm.
' Hoohoo ' or ' Oo ' of the natives of the Sandwich Islands.

Friendly Islands (*Lath.*) (?) ; Sandwich Islands (Owhyhee, Atoui or Atooi or Atowi or Towi or Attoway or Tauai or Kauai).

DREPANIS (VESTIARIA) COCCINEA.   B.M.

Mellisuga coccinea, Merr. Beitr. Vög. pl. 4.
Hook-billed Red Creeper, Lath. Gen. Syn. i. p. 704.
Certhia coccinea, Gmel. S. N. i. p. 470 ; Ellis's Icon. ined. 29.
Certhia vestiaria, Lath. Ind. Orn. i. p. 282.
Drepanis coccinea, G. R. Gray, Gen. of B. i. p. 96.
Drepanis vestiaria, Temm.
Melitreptus vestiarius, Vieill. Gal. des Ois. t. 181.
Nectarinia coccinea, Bloxh. Byron's Voy. p. 248.
Vestiaria evi, Less.
Vestiaria coccinea, Reichenb.
Vieill. Ois. dor. t. 52.
♀ *Hook-billed Green Creeper,* Lath. Gen. Syn. i. p. 703. pl. 33. f. 1.
Certhia obscura, Gmel. S. N. i. p. 470.
Drepanis obscura, Temm.
Melitreptus obscurus, Vieill. Encyc. Méth. p. 601.
Drepanis coccinea ♀?, Gray, Zool. Misc. p. 12.
' Hehivi ' or ' Olokele ' (*Bloxh.*), ' Eec-eve ' or ' Hcoro-taire ' of the natives.

Sandwich Islands (Owhyhee, Mowee or Maui, Whahoo or Woahoo or Oahu or Oahoo, Atoui).

DREPANIS (HIMATIONE) SANGUINEA.   B.M.

Crimson Creeper, Lath. Gen. Syn. i. p. 739.
Certhia sanguinea, Gmel. S. N. i. p. 479 ; Ellis's Icon. ined. 30 ; Vieill. Ois. dor. t. 66.
Nectarinia sanguinea, Cuv.
Drepanis sanguinea, G. R. Gray, Gen. of B. i. p. 96.
Nectarinia Byronensis, Bloxh. Byron's Voy. p. 249 ; Griff. Anim. Kingd. ii. p. 390, pl.
Himatione sanguinea, Cab. Mus. Heine, p. 99.
Petrodroma sanguinea, Vieill. N. Dict. Hist. Nat. xxvi. p. 108.
Myzomela? sanguinea, G. R. Gray.
Drepanis Byronensis, Gray, Zool. Misc. p. 12.
♀ *Olive-green Creeper,* Lath. Gen. Syn. i. p. 740.
Certhia virens, Gmel. S. N. i. p. 479 ; Ellis's Icon. ined. 31 ; Vieill. Ois. dor. t. 67, 68.
Melitreptus virens, Vieill. Encyc. Méth. p. 607.
Nectarinia flava, Bloxh. Byron's Voy. p. 249.
Phyllornis tonganensis, Less.
Phyllornis virens, G. R. Gray.

Himatione chloris, Cab. Mus. Heine, p. 99.
Drepanis flava, Gray, Zool. Misc. p. 12.
Himatione flava, Reichenb.
Juv. *Himatione maculata*, Cab. Mus. Heine, p. 100 ; Pr. B.
Compt. Rend. 1853, p. .
♂ 'Apapanie,' ♀ 'Amakee' of the natives.
Sandwich Islands.

DREPANIS (HEMIGNATHUS) ELLISIANA.

Certhia obscura, (nec Gmel.) Vieill. Ois. dor. t. 53 ?
Hemignathus obscurus, (nec Gmel.) Licht. Berl. Trans. 1838, t. v.
f. 1 ; Ellis's Icon. ined. 28 (1779).
Hemignathus? obscurus, Cass. U. S. Expl. Exped. 1858, p. 179.
' Jibi ' of the natives..
Sandwich Islands (Oahu).

DREPANIS (HEMIGNATHUS) LUCIDA.   B.M.

Hemignathus lucidus, Licht. Berl. Trans. 1838, t. v. f. 2, 3.
Hemignathus olivaceus, Licht. Voy. de la Vénus, Ois. t. 1.
Heterorhynchus olivaceus, Lafr. Mag. de Zool. 1839, t. x.
Vestiaria heterorhynchus, Less. Rev. Zool. 1842, p. 209.
Drepanis lucida, G. R. Gray, Gen. of B. i. p. 96.
Sandwich Islands (Oahu).

MOHO NOBILIS.   B.M.

Yellow-tufted Bee-eater, Lath. Gen. Syn. i. p. 683.
Gracula nobilis, Merr. Vögel, t. 11.
Merops niger, Gmel. S. N. i. p. 465 ; Ellis's Icon. ined. 26.
Merops fasciculatus, Lath. Ind. Orn. i. p. 275.
Philemon fasciculatus, Vieill. Encyc. Méth. p. 613.
Ptiloturus fasciculatus, Peale, U. S. Expl. Exped. p. 148.
Epimachus pacificus, Licht.
Moho nigra, G. R. Gray, Gen. of B. i. p. 96.
Moho nobilis, Cass. U. S. Expl. Exped. 1858, p. 170.
Moho fasciculata, Less. Tr. d'Orn. p. 302.
Mohoa fasciculata, Reichenb.
Meliphaga fasciculata, Temm. Pl. Col. 471.
Acrulocercus niger, Cab.
Acrulocercus pacificus, Licht. Nomencl. p. 54.
Nectarinia niger, Bloxh.
Var. *Yellow-tufted Bee-eater*, var. A, Dixon's Voy. pl. 19.
' Uho ' and ' Oo ' of the natives.
Sandwich Islands (Owhyhee).

MOHO BRACCATA.

Moho braccata, Cass.
Hab. —— ?

NECTARINIA FLAVIGASTRA.

Nectarinia flavigastra, Gould, Proc. Z. S. 1843, p. 104; Zool. of Sulph. pl. 24.

New Ireland.

DICÆUM RUBRUM.

Scarlet Creeper, Lath. Gen. Syn. i. p. 740.
Certhia rubra, Gmel. S. N. i. p. 479 ; Vieill. Ois. dor. t. 54.
Dicæum atripes, Vieill. N. Dict. Hist. Nat. ix. p. 408.
Dicæum scarlatinum, Schinz.
Dicæum rubrum, G. R. Gray, Gen. of B. i. p. 100.
Cardinal Honey-eater, ♀, Lath. Hist. of B. iv. p. 199.

One of the Islands in the South Seas.

DICÆUM ÆNEUM.

Dicæum æneum, Homb. & Jacq.Voy.au Pôle Sud,i.p. 97.t. 22.f.1.

Solomon Islands (St. George).

MELIPHAGIDÆ.

MYZOMELA CARDINALIS.   B.M.

Cardinal Creeper, Lath. Gen. Syn. i. p. 733. pl. 33. f. 2.
Certhia cardinalis, Forst. Descr. &c. p. 262; G. Forst. Icon. ined.
63 ; Gmel. S. N. i. p. 472.
Nectarinia cardinalis, Steph.
Melitreptus cardinalis, pt., Vieill. Encyc. Méth. p. 604.
Meliphaga cardinalis, pt., Vig. & Horsf.
Phylidonyris sanguinea, Less.
Myzomela melanogastra, Pr. B. Compt. Rend. 1854, p. 263.
'Kuyaméta' of the natives of Tanna (*Forst.*).

New Hebrides (Erromango, Aneiteum, Tanna).

Juv. Olive-brown, with some scarlet feathers on back, and slightly tinged on the rump with scarlet ; greater wing-coverts, quills, and tail slightly margined with yellow ; beneath fuscous-yellow, but yellowish-white in middle of abdomen and on side of breast next the shoulder ; front and throat scarlet, varied on the latter with yellow.

? MYZOMELA PUSILLA.

Certhia cardinalis, (Gmel.) Vieill. Ois. dor. t. 58.
Hab. ――?

This bird is recorded by Vieillot as being only 3½ inches in length, and therefore much smaller than the preceding species.

MYZOMELA NIGRIVENTRIS.   B.M.

Myzomela nigriventris, Peale, U. S. Expl. Exped. p. 150. t. 12. f. 1.

Myzomela rubrater, (nec Less.) Hartl. Wiegm. Arch. für Naturg. 1852, p. 131.
Myzomela Arnouxi, Verr.

Samoan or Navigators' Islands; Society Islands; Sandwich Islands.

MYZOMELA RUBRATRA.

Cinnyris rubrater, Less. Man. ii. p. 55 ; Kittl. Kupf.Vög. t. 8. f. 1.
Myzomela rubratra, Pr. B. Compt. Rend. 1854, p. 263.
Myzomela sanguinolenta, pt., G. R. Gray, Gen. of B. i. p. 118.

Ladrone or Marian Islands (Guam or Guahan or Guacam); Pelew or Pellew or Palaos Islands; Island of Vanikoro?

MYZOMELA MAJOR. B.M.

Myzomela major, Pr. B. Compt. Rend. 1854, p. 264.
Caroline Islands (Oualan).

MYZOMELA CHERMESINA. B.M.

Myzomela chermesina, G. R. Gray, Gen. of B. i. pl. 38.
Hab. ——?

MYZOMELA JUGULARIS. B.M.

Myzomela jugularis, Peale, U. S. Expl. Exped. p. 150. pl. 12. f. 2.
Myzomela solitaria, Jacq. & Pucher. Voy. au Pôle Sud, i. p. 99. t. 22. f. 6.
Feejee Islands.

MYZOMELA LAFARGEI.

Myzomela Lafargei, Homb. & Jacq. Voy. au Pôle Sud, i. p. 98. t. 22. f. 5.
Solomon Islands.

MYZOMELA? ——?

"*Souimanga à gorge bronzée,*" Less. & Garn. Voy. de la Coqu. Zool. i. p. 344.
' Sic sic ' of the natives.
New Ireland (Port Praslin).

Note.—Another species probably belonging to this genus is also mentioned under the name of
"*Souimanga rouge et gris,*" Quoy & Gaim. Voy. de l'Astrol. Zool. i. p. 162.
Island of Vanikoro.

GLYCIPHILA POLIOTIS. B.M.

Glyciphila poliotis, G. R. Gray, Proc. Z. S. 1859, p. 160.
Loyalty Islands.

GLYCIPHILA MODESTA.   B.M.

Glyciphila modesta, G. R. Gray, Proc. Z. S. 1859, p. 160.
New Caledonia (Island of Nu).

GLYCIPHILA? CHLOROPHÆA.

Certhia chlorophaea, Forst. Descr. &c. p. 264.
—— ? *chlorophæa*, G. R. Gray, Proc. Z. S. 1859, p. 160.
New Caledonia.

GLYCIPHILA? INCANA.

New Caledonian Creeper, Lath. Gen. Syn. ii. p. 161.
Certhia incana, Lath. Ind. Orn. p. 296.
—— ? *incana*, G. R. Gray, Proc. Z. S. 1859, p. 160.
New Caledonia.

MELIPHAGA? FUSCA.

Brown Creeper, Lath. Gen. Syn. i. p. 732.
Certhia fusca, Gmel. S. N. i. p. 472; Vieill. Ois. dor. t. 65.
Petrodroma fusca, Vieill. N. Dict. Hist. Nat. xxvi. p. 107.
Melitreptus fuscus, Vieill. N. Dict. Hist. Nat. xiv. p. 304.
One of the South Sea Islands.

MELIPHAGA? FASCIATA.

Certhia fasciata, Forst. Descr. &c. p. 263.
—— ? *fasciata*, G. R. Gray, Proc. Z. S. 1859, p. 160.
Certhia undulata, Sparrm. Mus. Carls. t. 34?
New Caledonia.

MELIPHAGA? OLIVACEA.

Merops olivaceus, Shaw, Gen. Zool. viii. p. 180; Vieill. Ois. dor.
(Prom.) t. 5.
Furnarius olivaceus, Steph.
Philemon olivaceus, Vieill. N. Dict. Hist. Nat. xxvii. p. 431.
Drepanis olivacea, G. R. Gray.
One of the Islands in the South Seas.

MELIPHAGA (SARCOGENYS) CARUNCULATA.   B.M.

Wattled Creeper, Lath. Gen. Syn. i. p. 732.
Certhia carunculata, Forst. Descr. &c. p. 165; G. Forst. Icon.
ined. 64; Gmel. S. N. i. p. 472; Vieill. Ois. dor. t. 69 & 70, var.
Meliphaga? carunculata, G. R. Gray, Gen. of B. i. p. 122.
Creadion musicus, Vieill. Encyc. Méth. p. 875.
Myzantha carunculata, Hartl. Wiegm. Arch. für Naturg. 1852,
p. 130.
Ptilotis carunculata, Cass.
Xanthotis carunculata, Reichenb.

Philedon chrysotis, Cuv.
'Foulehaio' or 'Fureehee-òw' of the natives of the Tonga Islands.
'Eyow' of the natives of the Samoan Islands.

Tonga Islands (Eaoowe or Eooa or Eoa or Middleburg, Tongatabu) ; Feejee Islands ; Samoan or Navigators' Islands.

ANTHOCHÆRA? ANGUSTIPLUMA.

Entomiza? *angustipluma*, Peale, U. S. Expl. Exped. p. 147.
Anthochæra? *angustipluma*, Hartl. Wiegm. Arch. für Naturg.
1852, p. 131.
Moho angustipluma, Cass. U. S. Expl. Exped. 1858, p. 168. pl. 11.
f. 1.
Moho atriceps, Less. Tr. d'Orn. p. 646 ?

Society Islands (Hawaii or Owhyhee).

TROPIDORHYNCHUS LESSONI. B.M.

Tropidorhynchus diemenensis, Less. Tr. d'Orn. p. 401; Pucher.
Arch. du Mus. 1855, p.   . t. 21.
Tropidorhynchus Lessoni, G. R. Gray, Proc. Z. S. 1859, p. 161.

New Caledonia (Port St. Vincent, Isle of Pines) ; Loyalty Islands.

TROPIDORHYNCHUS (LEPTORNIS) SAMOENSIS.

Merops samoensis, Homb. & Jacq. Ann. des Sci. Nat. n. s. xvi.
p. 314.
Entomiza? *olivacea*, Peale, U. S. Expl. Exped. p. 145.
Leptornis sylvestris, Jacq. & Pucher. Voy. au Pôle Sud, i. p. 86.
t. 17. f. 1.
Leptornis samoensis, Hartl. Wiegm. Arch. für Naturg. 1852,
p. 130.

Samoan or Navigators' Islands.

CERTHIADÆ.

TATARE OTAITIENSIS. B.M.

Sitta caffra, Sparrm. Mus. Carls. t. 4.
Oriolus musæ, Forst. Descr. &c. p. 163 ; G. Forst. Icon. ined. 55.
Sitta otatare, Less. Voy. de la Coqu. i. p. 666. t. 23. f. 2.
Tatare otaitiensis, Less. Tr. d'Orn. p. 317.
Tatarea longirostris, Reichenb.
Tatare fuscus, Less. Rev. Zool. 1842, p. 210 (juv. ?).
Ellis's Icon. ined. 76.
'O-tatare' of the natives of the Society Islands.
'Komako' of the natives of the Marquesas Islands.

Society Islands (Ulietea or Oriadea, Tahiti) ; Low or Paumotu or Pomotou Islands (Carlshoff or Aratica, &c.) ; Samoan or Navigators' Islands ; Tonga Islands (Tongatabu) ; Marquesas Islands.

(?) Tatare longirostris.

Long-billed Thrush, Lath. Gen. Syn. ii. p. 67.
Turdus longirostris, Gmel. S. N. i. p. 823.
Tatare longirostris, G. R. Gray, List of Gen. of B. 1840, p. 24.
Hybristes longirostris, Sundev.
Society Islands (Eimeo or Emao or York Island).

Tatare syrinx.

Sylvia syrinx, Kittl. Mém. Acad. St. Petersb. ii. p. 6. t. 6.
Tatare syrinx, Hartl. Wiegm. Arch. für Naturg. 1852, p. 131 ;
Voy. au Pôle Sud, t. 20. f. 5.
Eparnates syrinx, Reichenb.
Caroline Islands (Ualan or Oualan).

Tatare luscinia.

Thryothorus luscinius, Quoy & Gaim. Voy. de l'Astrol. i. p. 202.
t. 5. f. 2.
Tatare luscinia, G. R. Gray, Gen. of B. App. p. 8.
Hybristes luscinia, Reichenb.
' Gapio ' of the natives.
Ladrone or Marian Islands.

Tatare? æquinoctialis.

Sylvia æquinoctialis, Lath. Ind. Orn. ii. p. 553.
Christmas Island.

LUSCINIDÆ.

Note.—Quoy and Gaimard have recorded (Voy. de l'Uranie, Zool.
i. p. 36) that " *Petits figuiers d'un vert jaunâtre* " are found at
the Sandwich Islands.

Saxicola (?) luctuosa.

Saxicola luctuosa, Müll. ; Pr. B. Consp. Av. i. p. 304.
Samoan or Navigators' Islands (*Pr. B.*).

Saxicola(?) merula.

Saxicola merula, Less. & Garn. Voy. de la Coqu. Zool. i. p. 662.
New Ireland (Port Praslin).

Note.—Quoy and Gaimard notice (Voy. de l'Astrol. Zool. i. p.150)
that a " *Traquet* " was found at Tongatabu ; but no description is
given of it.

Petroica pusilla.

Petroica pusilla, Peale, U. S. Expl. Exped. p. 202. t. 9. f. 4.
Samoan or Navigators' Islands.

PETROICA SIMILIS. B.M.

Fuscous-black ; spot on frontlet, a large space on wing-coverts, sides and under tail-coverts, white ; breast and abdomen scarlet.

Very like *Petroica pusilla* of Peale, from Navigators' Islands, but it is larger (being $4\frac{1}{2}''$ in length), with the throat varied with white, scarlet, and fuscous-black ; the outer tail-feather white, with a blackish spot near the apex, and the outer margin only of the second feather white.

New Hebrides (Aneiteum).

PETROICA FORSTERI.

Turdus minutus, Forst. Descr. &c. pp. 84, 257.
Petroica ——?, G. R. Gray, Proc. Z. S. 1859, p. 161.
Isle of Pines.

ACANTHIZA FLAVOLATERALIS. B.M.

Acanthiza flavolateralis, G. R. Gray, Proc. Z. S. 1859, p. 161.
New Caledonia (Island of Nu).

ACANTHIZA? ——?

Fauvette, Less. Voy. de la Coqu. Zool. i. p. 433.
Caroline Islands (Oualan).

ZOSTEROPS FLAVIFRONS. B.M.

Yellow-fronted Flycatcher, Lath. Gen. Syn. ii. p. 342.
Muscicapa heteroclita, G. Forst. Descr. &c. p. 271 ; Icon. ined. 158.
Muscicapa flavifrons, Lath. Ind. Orn. i. p. 479.
Zosterops ——, Licht.
' Kelàb-lábbel ' of the natives of Tanna.
New Hebrides (Erromango, Aneiteum, Tanna).

ZOSTEROPS FLAVICEPS.

Zosterops flaviceps, Peale, U. S. Expl. Exped. p. 95. t. 10. f. 4.
Feejee Islands.

ZOSTEROPS GRISEONOTA. B.M.

Zosterops griseonota, G. R. Gray, Proc. Z. S. 1859, p. 161.
New Caledonia (Island of Nu).

ZOSTEROPS MELANOPS. B.M.

Zosterops melanops, G. R. Gray, MSS.

Back obscure grey ; head, wing-coverts, tail-coverts, and margins of quills and tail-feathers yellowish-green ; front, top of head, and cheeks varied with black ; throat yellow ; breast pale cinereous ;

abdomen and under tail-coverts cinereous-white; ring round the
eyes white; quills and tail fuscous-black.   Bill pale horn-colour.
  Length 5"; wings 2" 4'''.
  Loyalty Islands.

ZOSTEROPS XANTHOCHROA.   B.M.
  Zosterops xanthochroa, G. R. Gray, Proc. Z. S. 1859, p. 161.
  New Caledonia (Island of Nu).

ZOSTEROPS CONSPICILLATA.
  Zosterops conspicillata, G. R. Gray, Gen. of B. i. p. 198.
  Dicæum conspicillatum, Kittl. Mém. Acad. St. Petersb. 1835, ii.
t. 4; id. Kupf. Vög. t. 19. f. 1.
  Ladrone or Marian Islands (Guam).

ZOSTEROPS CINEREA.
  Drepanis cinerea, Kittl. Mém. Acad. St. Petersb. 1835, t. 5; id.
Kupf. Vög. t. 8. f. 2.
  Zosterops cinerea, Hartl. Wiegm. Arch. für Naturg. 1852, p. 131.
  Diceum cinereum, G. R. Gray, Gen. of B. i. 1. p. 100.
  Caroline Islands (Oualan).

                          TURDIDÆ.

TURDUS (MERULA) VANIKORENSIS.   B.M.
  Turdus vanikorensis, Quoy & Gaim. Voy. de l'Astrol. i. p. 188.
t. 7. f. 2.
  Merula vanikorensis, Cass. U. S. Expl. Exped. (1858) p. 158.
  Geocichla vanikorensis, Pr. B. Consp. Av. i. p. 268.
  Island of Vanikoro ; Samoan or Navigators' Islands (Upolu).

TURDUS (MERULA) XANTHOPUS.   B.M.
  Turdus xanthopus, Forst. Descr. &c. p. 266 ; G. Forst. Icon. ined.
151.
  'Degbé' of the natives.
  New Caledonia (Island of Nu).

  The *Merula vinitincta* of Mr. Gould, from Lord Howe's Island, is
closely allied to this species.

TURDUS (MERULA) ULIETENSIS.
  Bay Thrush, Lath. Gen. Syn. ii. p. 35.
  Turdus badius, Forst. Descr. &c. p. 239 ; G. Forst. Icon. ined.
146.
  Turdus ulietensis, Gmel. S. N. i. p. 815.
  'Eboonàe-nou-nou' of the natives.
  Society Islands (Oriadea or Ulietea).

Note.—Latham has given the following species as from the Sandwich Islands :—

Lanius melanocephalus, Gmel. S. N. i. p. 309 ;
Pycnonotus melanocephalus, G. R. Gray ;

but it has since been found to be from Malacca.

MUSCICAPIDÆ.

RHIPIDURA LESSONI.

Monarcha cinerea, Peale, U. S. Expl. Exped. p. 101.
Rhipidura Lessoni, G. R. Gray, Gen. of B. i. p. 258.
Leucocerca Lessoni, Pr. B. Consp. Av. i. p. 324.
Muscylva Lessoni, Homb. & Jacq. Voy. au Pôle Sud, i. p. 75. t. 11. f. 2.

Feejee Islands (Viti Levu).

RHIPIDURA —— ?

Muscicapa ventilabrum, var., Forst. Descr. &c. pp. 87 & 256.

New Hebrides (Tanna).

RHIPIDURA NEBULOSA.

Rhipidura nebulosa, Peale, U. S. Expl. Exped. p. 99. pl. 9. f. 2.

Samoan or Navigators' Islands (Upolu).

RHIPIDURA PECTORALIS.

Muscylva pectoralis, Homb. & Jacq. Voy. au Pôle Sud, i. p. 75. t. 11. f. 3. 3.
Rhipidura pectoralis, G. R. Gray, Gen. of B. i. p. 258.

Island of Vanikoro ; Ladrone or Marian Islands ?

RHIPIDURA SETOSA.

Muscipeta setosa, Quoy & Gaim. Voy. de l'Astrol. i. p. 181. t. 4. f. 4.
Rhipidura setosa, G. R. Gray, Gen. of B. i. p. 259.

New Ireland (Carteret Harbour).

RHIPIDURA TRICOLOR.   B.M.

Muscicapa tricolor, Vieill. N. Dict. Hist. Nat. xxi. p. 490.
Muscipeta melanoleuca, Quoy & Gaim. Voy. de l'Astrol. i. p.180. t. 4. f. 3.
Rhipidura melanoleuca, G. R. Gray, Gen. of B. i. p. 259.
Sauloprocta melanoleuca, Cab. Mus. Ornith. Hein. p. 57.
' Rouquine' of the natives.

New Ireland (Carteret Harbour, Port Praslin).

MYIAGRA VANIKORENSIS.   B.M.

Platyrhynchus vanikorensis, Quoy & Gaim. Voy. de l'Astrol. i. p. 183. t. 5. f. 1.

Platygnathus vanikorensis, Hartl.Wiegm. Arch. für Naturg.1852, p. 132.
Muscicapa vanikorensis, G. R. Gray, Gen. of B. i. p. 262.
Myiagra vanikorensis, Cass. U. S. Expl. Exped. (1858) p. 148.
Island of Vanikoro ; Feejee Islands.

MYIAGRA VIRIDINITENS.   B.M.
Myiagra viridinitens, G. R. Gray, Proc. Z. S. 1859, p. 162.
Loyalty Islands.

MYIAGRA MELANURA.   B.M.
It is in general appearance like *M. viridinitens*, but the outer
margin of the outer tail-feather is not, nor are the tips of the first,
second and third feathers, white. They are but slightly margined
on the inner edge and at the tips with white.
♀. Greyish-brown on back ; head and rump plumbeous ; wings
and tail-feathers fuscous-black ; throat and abdomen white tinged
with rufous ; breast rufous.
Length 5″ 4‴ ; wings 2″ 11‴.
New Hebrides (Erromango, Aneiteum).

MYIAGRA OCEANICA.
Myiagra oceanica, Homb. & Jacq. Voy. au Pôle Sud, i. p. 77.
t. 12*. f. 1, 2.
Hogole or Hogoleu or Torres Islands.

MYIAGRA CALEDONICA.   B.M.
Myiagra caledonica, Pr. B. Rev. et Mag. de Zool. 1857, p. 49.
Myiagra perspicillata, G. R. Gray, Proc. Z. S. 1859, p. 161 ?
New Caledonia.

MYIAGRA ALBIVENTRIS.
Platyrhynchus albiventris, Peale, U. S. Expl. Exped. p. 102.
Platygnathus albiventris, Hartl. Wiegm. Arch. für Naturg. 1852,
p. 132.
Myiagra rubecula, (Lath.) Cass. U.S. Expl. Exped. 1858, p. 149.
Samoan or Navigators' Islands.

MYIAGRA MODESTA.   B.M.
Like *M. latirostris*, Gould, but smaller in size ; the bill is not so
wide at the base, and more gradually narrowed towards the tip ;
the throat white, slightly tinged with rufous ; the tail plumbeous-
grey, with the tips of the feathers (except the two middle ones)
narrowly margined with white.
Length 5″ 9‴ ; wings 2″ 9‴.
New Ireland.

? TCHITREA ——— ?

Muscicapa (Tchitrea) cristata, (Gm.) Less. Tr. d'Orn. p. 386.
Ladrone or Marian Islands.

PIEZORHYNCHUS LUCIDA ?

" *Gobe mouche*," Garn. Voy. de la Coqu. Zool. i. p. 344.
Piezorhynchus lucida, G. R. Gray, Cat. of Birds of New Guinea,
B.M. p. 27 ?
'Tenourikine' of the natives.
New Ireland (Port Praslin).

PIEZORHYNCHUS CHALYBEOCEPHALA.

Muscicapa chalybeocephala, Garn. Voy. de la Coqu. t. 15. f. 2.
Piezorhynchus chalybeocephala, G. R. Gray, P. Z. S. 1859, p. 161.
New Ireland. (New Guinea, B.M.)

MONARCHA CASTANEIVENTRIS.   B.M.

Monarcha castaneiventris, Verr. Rev. et Mag. de Zool. 1858, p. .

♂. Shining black ; wings and tail fuscous-black ; abdomen, under
wing-coverts and vent rufous-castaneous.
Length 9″.
Samoan or Navigators' Islands.

MONARCHA (POMAREA) NIGRA.   B.M.

Society Flycatcher, Lath. Gen. Syn. Suppl. p. 174.
Muscicapa atra, Forst. Descr. &c. p. 170.
Muscicapa nigra, Sparrm. Mus. Carls. t. 23 ; Gmel. S. N. i. p.747.
Luteous Flycatcher, Lath. Gen. Syn. iii. p. 342.
Muscicapa lutea, Gmel. S. N. i. p. 944 ; Forst. Icon. ined. 156.
Muscicapa pomarea, Less. Man. d'Orn. i. p. 192.
Muscicapa maupitiensis, Garn. Voy. Coqu. i. p. 592. t. 17.
Monarcha nigra, G. R. Gray, Gen. of B. i. p. 260.
Pomarea nigra, Pr. B. Compt. Rend. 1854, p. 650.
♂ 'Mamao,' ♀ 'Oomamao' of the natives of the Society Islands.
♂ 'Patiateo,' ♀ 'Koksovia' of the natives of the Marquesas
Islands.
'Tehikibèeoo' or 'Dengha-Dengha' of the natives of the Tonga
Islands.
Society Islands (Otaheite, Maurau or Marna or Maupiti or Mau-
pili) ; Tonga Islands (Tongatabu) ; Marquesas Islands (Waitahoo).

MONARCHA (METABOLUS) RUGENSIS.   B.M.

Muscicapa rugensis, Homb. & Jacq. Ann. des Sci. N. n. s. xvi.
p. 312.
Monarcha rugensis, Hartl. Wiegm. Arch. für Naturg. 1852, p. 133.
Colluricincla rugensis, Pucher. Voy. au Pôle Sud, t. 13.
Metabolus rugensis, Pr. B. Compt. Rend. 1854, p. 650.
Caroline Islands.

MONARCHA (ARSES) CHRYSOMELA.

Muscicapa chrysomela, Garn. Voy. de la Coqu. t. 18. f. 2.
Arses chrysomela, Less.
' Pipimaloume' of the natives of New Ireland.
New Ireland. (New Guinea, B.M.)

AMPELIDÆ.

PACHYCEPHALA CHLORURUS.   B.M.

Very like *P. gutturalis*, Gould ; but the tail is yellowish-green,
varied with black, while the tips of the feathers are obscure grey.
The bill is intermediate in size between *P. gutturalis* and *P. mela-
nura*.
Length 6" 3‴.
New Hebrides (Erromango, Aneiteum).

PACHYCEPHALA VITIENSIS.   B.M.

Like *P. melanura*, Gould, but with the back and wing-coverts
dark olive, the greater wing-coverts only black, and the tertials
broadly margined with greyish-olive ; tail black, with the tips margined with greyish-olive. The bill is also rather less in size.
♀. Top of head plumbeous ; back, wing-coverts, and margins of
tertials dark olivaceous-brown ; quills and tail fuscous-black, the
latter margined with olive, and primaries with grey. Beneath the
body uniform rufous, paler towards the under tail-coverts.
Length 6" 3‴.
Feejee Islands (Island of Ngau).

PACHYCEPHALA ORIOLOIDES.   B.M.

Pachycephala orioloides, Pucher., Homb. & Jacq. Voy. au Pôle
Sud, i. p. 57. t. 5. f. 3.
Pachycephala astrolabi, Pr. B. Consp. Av. i. p. 329.
Solomon Islands.

PACHYCEPHALA DIADEMATA.

Eopsaltria icteroides, Peale, U. S. Expl. Exped. p. 97. pl.10. f.3.
Eopsaltria diademata, Pucher. Voy. au Pôle Sud, p. 55. t. 5. f. 1.
Pachycephala Hombroni, Pr. B. Consp. Av. i. p. 329.

Var. (?)   B.M.

Throat varied with greyish-brown and white ; the band from the
nostrils to the eyes white.
Samoan or Navigators' Islands.

(?) PACHYCEPHALA FLAVIFRONS.

Eopsaltria flavifrons, Peale, U. S. Expl. Exped. i. p. 96. pl.10. f.1.
Samoan or Navigators' Islands.

(?) PACHYCEPHALA ALBIFRONS.

Eopsaltria albifrons, Peale, U. S. Expl. Exped. p. 123. t. 10. f. 2.

Samoan or Navigators' Islands.

Peale remarks that probably these three are the same species; but the natives consider them as three distinct birds.

PACHYCEPHALA MELANOPS.

Eopsaltria melanops, Pucher., Homb. & Jacq. Voy. au Pôle Sud, i. p. 56. t. 5. f. 2.

Pachycephala Jacquinoti, Pr. B. Consp. Av. i. p. 329.

Tonga Islands (Vavao).

Note.—A 'Pie grièche,' which is probably a species of *Pachycephala*, is noticed by Quoy and Gaimard as found in Tongatabu (Voy. de l'Astrol. Zool. i. p. 159), but without any description.

PACHYCEPHALA XANTHETRAEA.   B.M.

Muscicapa xanthetraea, Forst. Descr. &c. p. 268.

Pachycephala xanthetraea, G. R. Gray, Proc. Z. S. 1859, p. 162.

'Màgga' of the natives.

New Caledonia (Island of Nu).

EOPSALTRIA CALEDONICA.   B.M.

Olive Flycatcher, Lath. Gen. Syn. ii. p. 342.

Muscicapa olivacea, G. Forst. Descr. &c. p. 271.

Muscicapa caledonica, Gmel. S. N. i. p. 944.

Eopsaltria? caledonica, G. R. Gray, Proc. Z. S. 1859, p. 162.

Eopsaltria variegata, G. R. Gray, Proc. Z. S. 1859, p. 162.

New Caledonia (Island of Nu).

EOPSALTRIA CUCULLATA.   B.M.   +

Top of head and ear-coverts rufous-brown; back, margins of quills, and tail, brownish-olive; beneath the body yellowish-white; throat white, with the feathers narrowly margined with rufous-brown; bill black; feet pale plumbeous.

Length 6" 3"'.

New Hebrides (Aneiteum).

EOPSALTRIA GAMBIERANA.

Lanius gambieranus, Less. Echo de M. S. 1844, p. 232.

Eopsaltria gambierana, Hartl. Wiegm. Arch. für Naturg. 1852, p. 133.

Low or Paumotu Islands (Gambier's Islands or Mangarewa).

EOPSALTRIA (CHASIEMPSIS) SANDWICHENSIS.   B.M.

Sandwich Flycatcher, Lath. Gen. Syn. ii. p. 344.

Muscicapa sandwichensis, Gmel. S. N. i. p. 945; Bloxh. Byron's Voy. p. 250.

Chasiempsis sandwicensis, Cab. Ornith. Notiz. i. p. 208.
' Erepeio' of the natives.
Sandwich Islands.

? EOPSALTRIA (CHASIEMPSIS) MACULATA.   B.M.

Spotted-winged Flycatcher, Lath. Gen. Syn. ii. p. 345.
Muscicapa maculata, Gmel. S. N. i. p. 945.
Ellis's Icon. ined. 87 (juv.).
Sandwich Islands.

EOPSALTRIA (CHASIEMPSIS) OBSCURA.

Dusky Flycatcher, Lath. Gen. Syn. ii. p. 344.
Muscicapa obscura, Gmel. S. N. i. p. 945.
Tænioptera obscura, Cass. U. S. Expl. Exped. 1858, p. 155. pl. 9.
f. 3.
Chasiempsis obscura, Hartl. Wiegm. Arch. für Naturg. 1852,
p. 133.
Phæornis obscura, Sclater, Ibis, 1859, p. 327.
Sandwich Islands (Owhyhee or Hawaii).

CAMPEPHAGA CALEDONICA.   B.M.

New Caledonian Crow, Lath. Gen. Syn. i. p. 377.
Corvus cinereus, Forst. Descr. &c. p. 260 ; G. Forst. Icon. ined. 53.
Corvus caledonicus, Gmel. S.N. i. p. 367.
Graucalus cæsius, Cuv., Pucher. Arch. du Mus. 1855, p. 323.
Pica cinerea, Wagl. Syst. Av.
Gazzola caledonica, Pr. B. Consp. Av. p. 383.
Campephaga caledonica, G. R. Gray, Gen. of B. p. 283.
' Ghewà ' of the natives of New Caledonia.
New Caledonia ; Isle of Pines ; New Hebrides (Erromango).

CAMPEPHAGA? ALBIFRONS.

Pacific Crow, Lath. Gen. Syn. i. p. 383.
Corvus pacificus, Gmel. S. N. i. p. 372.
Coracina albifrons, Vieill. Encyc. Méth. p. 771.
South Sea Islands (?).

CAMPEPHAGA (LALAGE) NÆVIA.

Nævous Flycatcher, Lath. Gen. Syn. ii. p. 343.
Muscicapa nævia, Forst. Descr. &c. p. 269 ; G. Forst. Icon. ined.
159 ; Gmel. S. N. i. p. 944.
Campephaga (Lalage) nævia, G. R. Gray, Proc. Z. S. 1859, p.163.
New Caledonia.

CAMPEPHAGA (LALAGE) PACIFICA.

Pacific Thrush, Lath. Gen. Syn. iii. p. 38.
Turdus pacificus, Gmel. S. N. i. p. 813 ; Hartl. Wiegm. Arch.
für Naturg. 1852, p. 130.

Ceblephyris karu, (Garn. & Less.) Quoy & Gaim. Voy. de l'Astrol.
Zool. i. p. 159?
Ellis, Icon. ined. 18.
Friendly Islands.

CAMPEPHAGA (LALAGE) MACULOSA.

Colluricincla maculosa, Peale, U. S. Expl. Exped. p. 81.
Lalage terat, (Bodd.) Cass. U. S. Expl. Exped. 1858, p. 143.
Lalage maculosa, Hartl. Wiegm. Arch. für Naturg. 1852, p. 132.
Feejee Islands; Samoan or Navigators' Islands (Upolu).

CAMPEPHAGA (LALAGE) KARU.

Ceblepyris karu, Less. Voy. Coqu. p. 633.
Notodela karu, Less. Tr. d'Orn. p. 374.
Lalage karu, Pr. B. Compt. Rend. 1854, p. 541.
'Karou' or 'Caru' of the natives.
New Ireland.

Note.—Ellis, in his *Icones ined.* 92, represents a bird from
Christmas Island, that appears to belong to the genus *Campephaga*
(*Lalage*), but which has not been recorded in any work that I am
acquainted with.

EDOLIUS COMICE.

Edolius comice, Less. & Garn. Voy. de la Coqu. Zool. i. p. 344.
New Ireland (Port Praslin).

ARTAMUS MELALEUCUS.   B.M.

Loxia melaleuca, Forst. Descr. &c. p. 272; G.Forst.Icon.ined.40.
Leptopteryx melaleuca, Wagl. Syst. Av. Lept. sp. 1.
Artamus melaleucus, G. R. Gray, Proc. Z. S. 1859, p. 163.
Artamus leucorhynchus, (Gm.).
Ocypterus berardi, Pr. B. Compt. Rend. 1854, p. 538.
'Keenh' of the natives.
New Caledonia (Island of Nu).

ARTAMUS ARNOUXI.

Ocypterus Arnouxi, Pr. B. Compt. Rend. 1854, p. 538.
New Caledonia?

ARTAMUS MENTALIS.   B.M.

Artamus mentalis, Jard. Ann. & Mag. N. H. xvi. p. 174. pl. 8.
Ocypterus mentalis, Peale, U. S. Expl. Exped. p. 84.
Artamus vitiensis, Homb. & Jacq. Voy. au Pôle Sud, i. p. 73. t. 9.
f. 1.
Feejee Islands.

LANIIDÆ.

COLLURICINCLA? SANDVICHENSIS.

Sandwich Thrush, Lath. Gen. Syn. iii. p. 39.
Turdus sandwichensis, Gmel. S. N. i. p. 813; Ellis's Icon. ined.
77; Bloxh. Byron's Voy. p. 250?
Tatare otaitiensis, pt., Cass. ? U. S. Expl. Exped. 1858, p. 158.
'Amauii' of the natives?
Sandwich Islands.

Note.—The *Lanius mystaceus*, Lath. Ind. Orn. Suppl. p. xix;
Levaill. Ois. d'Afr: t. 65 (*Laniarius mystaceus*, G. R. Gray, Gen. of
B. i. p. 299), has been stated by Levaillant to be from an isle in the
South Seas. It is, however, a made-up bird, being composed of a
portion of the *Lanius ferrugineus*, Gm., with the feathers on the belly
and tail from a species of red *Psittacus*, while the breast and vent
are those from a species of *Malaconotus*.

CORVIDÆ.

CORVUS AUSTRALIS.

South Sea Raven, Lath. Gen. Syn. i. p. 363.
Corvus australis, Gmel. S. N. i. p. 365. no. 21.
Corvus enca, (Horsf.) Wagl. Syst. Av. Corv. sp. 11.
Corvus coronoïdes, Vig. & Horsf.
Corvus coroneoides, Wagl.
'Coco' of the natives of New Ireland?
Friendly Islands; New Ireland?

CORVUS HAWAIIENSIS.

Corvus hawaiiensis, Peale, U. S. Expl. Exped. p. 106. pl. 6.
Corvus tropicus, (Gmel.) Bloxh. Byron's Voy. p. 249.
'Alala' of the natives.
Sandwich Islands (Hawaii or Owhyhee).

CORVUS ——?

Carrion Crow, pt., Lath. Gen. Syn. i. p. 370.
Corvus, n. sp., Licht., Forst. Descr. &c. p. 257.
Corvus corone, pt., Gmel. S. N. i. p. 365; Wagl. Syst. Av.
'Maga' of the natives.
New Caledonia.

CORVUS (PHYSOCORAX) MONEDULOIDES.

Corvus moneduloides, Less. Tr. d'Orn. p. 329.
Corvus inflatus, Temm. MSS.
Physocorax moneduloides, Pr. B. Compt. Rend. 1853, p. 829.
New Caledonia.

CORVUS (?) TROPICUS.

Tropic Crow, Lath. Gen. Syn. i. p. 384.
Corvus tropicus, Gmel. S. N. i. p. 372.
Cracticus ater, Vieill. N. Dict. d'Hist. Nat. v. p. 356.
Sandwich Islands (Owhyhee).

Note.—" An *Corvus* parvus remigibus cæruleis a cl. Cook in Nova Caledonia observatur ? "—*Wagl.* Syst. Av. under Pica, sp. 9; Cook's Voy. ii. p. 124.

The following bird has been recorded as from New Caledonia, viz. :—

Caledonian Crow, Lath. Gen. Syn. Suppl. ii. p. 116.
Corvus caledonicus, Lath. Ind. Orn. Suppl. p. xxv ; Labill. Voy. Atlas, t. 39.
Pica albicollis, Vieill. N. Dict. d'Hist. Nat. xxvi. p. 128.
Streptocitta caledonica, Pr. B. Consp. Av. i. p. 382.

It may be remarked that the specimens in the British Museum which agree with the description of the above-mentioned species are from Celebes, while Lesson states that this bird was obtained at the Island of Vanikoro by Quoy and Gaimard. The British Museum also contains the specimen from which Temminck gave his figure in Pl. Col. 444, under the name of *Garrula torquata*. This bird differs by its entirely black bill, the steel-blue glossiness of the plumage, the dull purple reflexion on the head, and the tail being rather shorter.

STURNIDÆ.

CHLAMYDERA (STURNOIDES) GIGAS.

Sturnoides gigas, Homb. & Jacq. Voy. au Pôle Sud, i. p. 84. t. 15. f. 2.
Samoan or Navigators' Islands.

CALORNIS (LAMPROCORAX) FULVIPENNIS.

Lamprotornis fulvipennis, Homb. & Jacq. Voy. au Pôle Sud, i. p. 81. t. 14. f. 2.
Lamprocorax fulvipennis, Pr. B. Compt. Rend. 1853, p. .
Solomon Islands (Sta Ysabel).

CALORNIS (LAMPROCORAX ?) CORVINA.   B.M.

Lamprotornis corvina, Kittl. Mém. Ac. de St. Pétersb. 1835, p. 7. t. 19 ; id. Kupf. Voy. t. 15. f. 3.
Calornis corvina, G. R. Gray, Gen. of B. App. p. 15.
Caroline Islands (Oualau).

CALORNIS PACIFICA.

Pacific Shrike, Lath. Gen. Syn. i. p. 164.
Lanius pacificus, Gmel. S. N. i. p. 306.
Calornis corvina, pt., Cass. U. S. Expl. Exped. 1858, p. 124 (?).
One of the islands in the South Seas.

CALORNIS ATROFUSCA.

Lamprotornis atrofusca, Peale, U. S. Expl. Exped. p. 109.
Aplonis atrofuscus, Hartl. Wiegm. Arch. für Naturg. 1852, p. 133.
Calornis corvina, pt., Cass. U. S. Expl. Exped. 1858, p. 124.
Samoan or Navigators' Islands (Tutuilla, Upolu).

CALORNIS NITIDA.   B.M.

Calornis nitida, G. R. Gray, Proc. Z. S. 1858, p. 181.
Lamprotornis metallicus, (Temm.) Garn. Voy. de la Coqu. Zool.
i. p. 343.
New Ireland.

CALORNIS OPACA.

Turdus columbinus, Gmel. S. N. i. p. 836 (?).
Calornis columbina, G. R. Gray (?).
Lamprotornis columbina, Kittl. Kupf. Voy. t. 15. f. 2.
Lamprotornis opaca, Licht. Mus. Heine, p. 201.
'Sali' of the natives of the Ladrone Islands.
'Ououaizai' of the natives of the Caroline Islands.
Ladrone or Marian Islands; Caroline Islands (Oualau).

APLONIS TABUENSIS.   B.M.

Tabuan Shrike, Lath. Gen. Syn. i. p. 164.
Lanius tabuensis, Gmel. S. N. i. p. 306.
Aplonis marginata, Gould, Proc. Z. S. 1836, p. 73.
Aplonis tabuensis, Hartl.
Aplonis marginalis, Hartl. Wiegm. Arch. für Naturg. 1852, p. 132.
Ellis's Icon. ined. 9.
Tonga Islands (Tongatabu).

APLONIS CASSINII.   B.M.

Lamprotornis fusca, Peale, U. S. Expl. Exped. p. 110. pl. 7. f. 1.
Aplonis marginata, Cass. U. S. Expl. Exped. 1858, p. 125.
Aplonis Cassinii, G. R. Gray, Proc. Z. S. 1859, p. 163.
Tonga Islands (Tongatabu) ; Feejee Islands.

APLONIS STRIATA.   B.M.

Blue-striped Roller, ♂, Lath. Gen. Syn. i. p. 414. pl. 16, low. fig.
Coracias pacifica, Forst. Descr. &c. p. 261 ; G. Forst. Icon. ined.
54, upp. fig.
Coracias striata, Gmel. S. N. i. p. 381.
Galgulus striatus, Vieill. N. Dict. Hist. Nat. xxix. p. 434.
Lanius striatus, Wagl.
Aplonis striata, G. R. Gray, Proc. Z. S. 1859, p. 163.
'Poorèp' of the natives.
New Caledonia (Island of Nu).

APLONIS BREVIROSTRIS.

Lamprotornis brevirostris, Peale, U. S. Expl. Exped. p. 111. pl. 7. f. 2.
Aplonis brevirostris, Hartl. Wiegm. Arch. für Naturg. 1852, p. 132.
Samoan or Navigators' Islands (Upolu).

APLONIS VIRIDIGRISEA. B.M.

Aplonis viridigrisea, G. R. Gray, Proc. Z. S. 1859, p. 164.
Blue-striped Roller, ♀, Lath. Gen. Syn. i. p. 414. pl. 16, upp. fig.
Coracias striata, ♀, Gmel. S. N. i. p. 381 (?); G. Forst. Icon. ined. 54, low. fig.
New Caledonia (Island of Nu).

APLONIS ATRONITENS. B.M.

Aplonis atronitens, G. R. Gray, Proc. Z. S. 1859, p. 164.
Loyalty Islands.

FRINGILLIDÆ.

ESTRELDA PSITTACEA. B.M.

Parrot Finch, Lath. Gen. Syn. ii. p. 287. pl. 48.
Fringilla pulchella, Forst. Descr. &c. p. 273; G. Forst. Icon. ined. 153.
Fringilla psittacea, Gmel. S. N. i. p. 48.
Estrelda psittacea, G. R. Gray, Gen. of B. ii. p. 369.
Erythrura psittacea, Pr. B. Consp. Av. p. 457.
Poëphila Paddoni, M'Gill. Ann. & Mag. N. H. 1858, ser. 3. vol. ii. p. 263.
Vieill. Ois. Chant. t. 32.
' Durubeèa' and ' Gherubeèa' of the natives of New Caledonia.
New Caledonia (Island of Nu); Sandwich Islands (?).

ESTRELDA TRICHROA.

Fringilla trichroa, Kittl. Mém. Acad. St. Pétersb. 1835, p. 8. t. 10.
Erythrura trichroa, Pr. B. Consp. Av. i. p. 457.
Estrelda trichura, G. R. Gray, Gen. of B. ii. p. 369.
Erythrura Kittlitzi, Pr. B.
Caroline Islands (Oualau).

AMADINA (ERYTHRURA) PEALII.

Geospiza prasina, Peale, U. S. Expl. Exped. p. 116.
Erythrura Pealei, Hartl. Wiegm. Arch. für Naturg. 1852, p. 132.
Feejee Islands (Venua Levu).

AMADINA (ERYTHRURA) CYANOVIRENS.

Geospiza cyanovirens, Peale, U. S. Expl. Exped. p. 117. pl. 8. f. 2.

Erythrura cyanovirens, Hartl. Wiegm. Arch. für Naturg. 1852, p. 132.

Samoan or Navigators' Islands (Upolu).

AMADINA (ERYTHRURA) PUCHERANI.

Erythrura Pucherani, Pr. B. Consp. Av. p. 457 ; Proc. Z. S. 1858, p. 462.

" In insulis Oceaniæ."

LOXOPS COCCINEA.   B.M.

Scarlet Finch, Lath. Gen. Syn. ii. p. 270.
Fringilla coccinea, Gmel. S. N. i. p. 921 ; Ellis's Icon. ined. 85.
Fringilla rufa, Bloxh. Byron's Voy. p. 250.
Linaria? *coccinea,* Gould, Voy. Sulphur, pl. 22.
Drepanis rufa, G. R. Gray, Gen. of B. i. p. 96.
Carduelis coccinea, Less. Compl. Buff. viii. p. 281.
Himatione rufa, Reichenb.
Hypoloxias coccinea, Licht. Pr. B. Consp. Av. i. p. 518.
Loxops coccinea, Cab. Ornith. Notiz. p. 330.
♀? *Fringilla sandwichensis,* Bloxh. Byron's Voy. p. 250.
Vieill. Ois. Chant. t. 31.
' Akepakepa ' of the natives.
Sandwich Islands.

LOXOPS INORNATA.   B.M.

Cactornis inornatus, Gould, Voy. Sulphur, pl. 25 ; Proc. Z. S. 1843, p. 104.

Low or Paumotu Islands (Bow or Harp Island, or Hau).

PSITTIROSTRA ICTEROCEPHALA.   B.M.

Parrot-billed Grosbeak, Lath. Gen. Syn. ii. p. 108. pl. 42.
Loxia psittacea, Gmel. S. N. i. p. 844 ; Ellis's Icon. ined. 79.
Psittirostra icterocephala, Temm. Pl. Col. 457.
Psittirostra sandwichensis, Steph.
Psittirostra psittacia, Swains. Classif. of B. ii. p. 295.
' Ohu' or ' Raouhi ' of the natives.
Sandwich Islands.

PSITTACIDÆ.

PLATYCERCUS (NYMPHICUS) CORNUTUS.   B.M.

Horned Parrot, Lath. Gen. Syn. i. p. 248. pl. 8.
Psittacus bisetis, Forst. Descr. &c. p. 258; G. Forst. Icon. ined. 43.
Psittacus cornutus, Gmel. S. N. i. p. 327.
Platycercus cornutus, Vigors, Zool. Journ. i. p. 522.
Nymphicus bisetis, Wagl. Monogr. Psitt. p. 522.
Nymphicus cornutus, G. R. Gray, List of Gen. of B. 1855, p. 86.
G. R. Gray & Mitch. Gen. of B. pl. 101.
' Kère ' or ' Kèghe' of the natives.
New Caledonia (South Harbour).

(?) PLATYCERCUS (―― ?) CALEDONICUS.

Caledonian Parrot, Lath. Gen. Syn. i. p. 248.
Psittacus caledonicus, Gmel. S. N. i. p. 328.
Psittacus bisetis, ♀, Shaw, Gen. Zool. viii. p. 452.
Platycercus caledonicus, Wagl. Monogr. Psitt. p. 532.
New Caledonia.

It is probably the female of *Platycercus cornutus.—Lath.*

(?) PLATYCERCUS CAPITATUS.

Psittacus capitatus, Shaw, Gen. Zool. viii. p. 466.
Red-hooded Parrot, Lath. Hist. of B. ii. p. 136.
Lori Perruche de la Mer Sud, Sonn.
Platycercus eximius, pt., Wagl. Monogr. Psitt. p. 530.

It is stated by Sonnini to be brought from the islands in the South
Seas.

PLATYCERCUS (CYANORAMPHUS) ERYTHRONOTUS.

Red-rumped Parrot, Lath. Gen. Syn. i. p. 249.
Psittacus novæ seelandiæ, Gmel. S. N. i. p. 328, nec Sparrm.
Psittacus zealandicus, Lath. Ind. Orn. i. p. 102.
Psittacus (Conurus) erythronotus, Kuhl, Consp. Psitt. pp. 7, 45.
Platycercus pacificus, Wagl. Monogr. Psitt. p. 524.
Platycercus erythronotus, Steph. Gen. Zool. xiv. p. 122.
Psittacus pacificus, Forst. Descr. &c. p. 238 ; G. Forst. Icon.
ined. 47.
Conurus phaëton, Des Murs, Rev. Zool. 1845, p. 449.
Platycercus phaëton, Des Murs, Iconogr. Ornith. t. 16.
Cyanoramphus pacificus, Pr. B. Rev. et Mag. de Zool. 1854,
p. 153.
Psittacus pacificus, var. γ, Gmel.
Psittacus (Conurus) novæ zealandiæ, var. 1, Kuhl.
'Aä Aä' of the natives.

Society Islands (Otaheite, Oriadea).

PLATYCERCUS (CYANORAMPHUS) ULIETANUS.   B.M.

Society Parrot, Lath. Gen. Syn. i. p. 250.
Psittacus ulietanus, Gmel. S. N. i. p. 328.
Psittacus (Conurus) ulietanus, Kuhl, Consp. Psitt. pp. 7, 44.
Platycercus ulietanus, Vig. Zool. Journ. i. p. 533, Suppl. pl. 3.
Cyanoramphus ulietanus, Pr. B. Rev. et Mag. de Zool. 1854,
p. 153.

Society Islands (Ulietea) ; New Hebrides (Tanna) (?).

Note.—Latham records as from New Caledonia, the

Pacific Parrot, var. C, Lath. Gen. Syn. i. p. 253.
Psittacus pacificus, var. δ, Gmel.
Psittacus auriceps, Kuhl, Consp. Psitt. sp. 69.
Platycercus auriceps, Vigors.

Kuhl, on the other hand, gives New Holland as its habitat ; but it is a species peculiar to New Zealand, from whence many specimens are brought.

PLATYCERCUS (PYRRHULOPSIS) HYSGINUS.

Psittacus hysginus, Forst. Descr. &c. p. 159; G. Forst. Icon. ined. 42.
Psittacus atropurpureus, Shaw, Mus. Lev. pl. p. 142 (?).
Platycercus tabuensis, Jard. & Selby, Ill. Orn. pl. 74.
Platycercus hysginus, Wagl. Monogr. Psitt. p. 540 (?).
Psittacus caledonicus, (Gmel.) Licht. Forst. Descr. &c. p. 159.
Conurus Anna, Bourj. St. Hil. Perr. t. 38.
Aprosmictus Anna, Cass. U. S. Expl. Exped. (1858) p. 236.
Ellis's Icon. ined. 11.
' Kāghākā ' of the natives of the Tonga Islands.

Tonga Islands (Eaoowe) ; Feejee Islands.

(?) PLATYCERCUS (PYRRHULOPSIS) TABUENSIS.   B.M.

Tabuan Parrot, Lath. Gen. Syn. i. p. 214. pl. 7.
Psittacus tabuensis, Gmel. S. N. i. p. 317.
Platycercus atrogularis, Peale, U. S. Expl. Exped. p. 129.
Platycercus tabuensis, Lear's Parr. pl. 16 (?).
Aprosmictus tabuensis, Pr. B. Rev. et Mag. de Zool. 1854, p. 153.

Tonga Islands (Tongatabu) ; Feejee Islands.

Some authors are of opinion that this bird is only the female of the preceding species.

PLATYCERCUS (PYRRHULOPSIS) SPLENDENS.

Platycercus splendens, Peale, U.S. Expl. Exped. p. 127. pl. 20. f. 1.
Aprosmictus splendens, Pr. B.

Feejee Islands (Viti Levu).

PLATYCERCUS (PYRRHULOPSIS) PERSONATUS.   B.M.

Coracopsis (?) *personatus,* G. R. Gray, Proc. Z. S. 1848, pl. 3.
Platycercus splendens, ♀ juv., Peale, U. S. Expl. Exped. p. 128.
pl. 20. f. 2.
Pyrrhulopsis personata, Reichenb.
Prosopeia personata, Pr. B.
Aprosmictus splendens, pt., Pr. B.
Aprosmictus personatus, Cass. U. S. Expl. Exped. 1858, p. 239.
Feejee Islands.

Note.—G. Forster, in his Account of the Voyage (ii. p. 334), speaks of large and beautiful Parroquets that were found in Tanna ; and he further describes them as having a black, red, and yellow plumage. This species has not been noticed in any other work.

The *Psittacus platurus,* Temm. & Kuhl, Consp. Psitt. p. 43 ;
    Prioniturus platurus, Wagl. Monogr. Psitt. p. 423 ;
was considered by Temminck as a resident of New Caledonia, but
has since been recorded by him as from Timor, &c.

The following bird has been recorded by various authors as from
the Sandwich Islands, viz.—

    Psittacus pyrrhopterus, Lath. Ind. Orn. Suppl. p. xxxii.
    Brotogeris pyrrhopterus, Vigors, Zool. Journ. ii. p. 400. pl. 4,
Suppl.
    Trichoglossus pyrrhopterus, Wagl. Monogr. Psitt. p. 547 ; Hartl.
Wiegm. Arch. für Naturg. 1852, p. 133.
    Conurus (Brotogeris) pyrrhopterus, G. R. Gray, List of Psitt.
B.M. p. 46.
but it seems peculiar to Guayaquil,' and may be taken from thence
to the previous-mentioned islands and so brought to Europe.

CHARMOSYNA PAPUENSIS.

Psittacus japonicus, Linn. S. N. i. p. 141.
Psittacus papuensis, Gmel. S. N. i. p. 317.
Charmosyna papuensis, Wagl. Monogr. Psitt. p. 555.
New Ireland (Carteret Harbour).

LORIUS CHLOROCERCUS.   B.M.

Lorius chlorocercus, Gould, Proc. Z. S. 1856, p. 137.
Solomon Islands (San Christoval).

LORIUS TRICOLOR.

Psittacus lory, Linn. S. N. i. p. 145 ; Voy. de la Coqu. Zool. i.
p. 342.
Lorius tricolor, Steph. Gen. Zool. xiv. p. 132.
New Ireland (Port Praslin).

EOS CARDINALIS.

Lorius cardinalis, Homb. & Jacq. Voy. au Pôle Sud, i. p. 103.
t. 24*. f. 2.
Eos cardinalis, Pr. B. Compt. Rend. 1857, p. 539.
Solomon Islands.

CORIPHILUS TAITIANUS.   B.M.

Otaheitan Blue Parrakeet, Lath. Gen. Syn. i. p. 255.
Psittacus sapphirinus, Forst. Descr. &c. p. 201.
Psittacus taitianus, Gmel. S. N. i. p. 329.
Psittacus porphyrio, Shaw, Nat. Misc. pl. 7.
Psittacus (Psittacula) taitianus, Kuhl, Consp. Psitt. pp. 9, 68.
Trichoglossus? *taitianus,* Steph. Gen. Zool. xiv. p. 130.
Brotogeris sappherinus, Swains. Classif. B. ii. p. 303.

Coriphilus sapphirinus, Wagl. Monogr. Psitt. p. 563.
Coriphilus notatus (!), G. R. Gray, Gen. of B. ii. p. 417.
Coriphilus taitianus, Pr. B. Rev. et Mag. de Zool. 1854, p. 157.
Levaill. Perr. t. 65.
Juv. *Psittacus cyaneus*, Sparrm. Mus. Carls. t. 27.
Psittacus sparrmanni, Bechst. Lath. Uebers. d. Vögel, p. 80.
Psittacus (Psittacula) Sparrmanni, Kuhl, Consp. Psitt. pp. 9, 68.
Brotogeris Sparrmanni, Steph. Gen. Zool. xiv. p. 133.
Coriphilus cyaneus, Wagl. Monogr. Psitt. p. 564.
Coriphilus taitianus, pt., Pr. B. Rev. et Mag. de Zool. 1854, p. 157.
Ellis's Icon. ined. 14.
' Vini ' or ' E-vini ' or ' Winnee ' or ' Venee ' of the natives.
Society Islands (Otaheite, Huahine or Huabane, Eimeo).

CORIPHILUS SMARAGDINUS.   B.M.

Psittaculus smaragdinus, Homb. & Jacq. Ann. des Sci. N. n. s.
xvi. p. 318.
Coriphilus dryas, Gould, Proc. Z. S. 1842, p. 165 ; Voy. of Sulph.
pl. 26.
Coriphilus Gouphili, Homb. & Jacq. Voy. au Pôle Sud, t. 24*. f. 3.
Krusenst. Voy. t. 17. f. .
' Pihiti ' of the natives.
Marquesas Islands (Noukahiva or Nunhiva or Nooaheevah or
Nooheiva or Federal Island).

CORIPHILUS SOLITARIUS.   B.M.

Psittacus solitarius, Lath. Ind. Orn. Suppl. xxiii.
Psittacus Phigys, Bechst. Lath. Uebers. d. Vög. p. 81.
Psittacus Levaillantii, Shaw, Nat. Misc. pl. 109.
Psittacus coccineus, Shaw, Gen. Zool. viii. p. 472.
Psittacus (Psittacula) Phigy, Kuhl, Consp. Psitt. pp. 9, 69.
Brotogeris? Phigy, Steph. Gen. Zool. xiv. p. 133.
Coriphilus solitarius, Wagl. Monogr. Psitt. p. 565.
Brotogeris coccineus, Swains. Classif. of B. ii. p. 303.
Lorius phigy, Less. Tr. d'Orn. p. 193.
Levaill. Perr. t. 64.
Feejee Islands (Ovolau, Viti Levu) ; Tonga Islands (Tongatabu).

CORIPHILUS KUHLII.   B.M.

Psittacula Kuhlii, Vigors, Zool. Journ. i. p. 412. pl. 16 ; Lears,
Parr. pl. 38.
Coriphilus Kuhlii, Wagl. Monogr. Psitt. p. 566.
Vini? coccineus, Less. Illustr. de Zool. t. 28.
Lorius Kuhlii, Less. Tr. d'Orn. p. 193.
Psittacula interfringillacea, Bourj. Perr. t. 83.
Brotogeris Kuhlii, Swains. Classif. of B. ii. p. 303.
' Ari-manou ' of the natives of the Society Islands.
Society Islands (Borabora) ; Sandwich Islands.

CORIPHILUS FRINGILLACEUS. B.M.

Blue-crested Parrakeet, Lath. Gen. Syn. i. p. 254.
Psittacus australis, Gmel. S. N. i. p. 329.
Psittacus fringillaceus, Gmel. S. N. i. p. 337.
Psittacus fringillarius, Lath. Ind. Orn. i. p. 112.
Psittacus pipilans, Lath. Ind. Orn. i. p. 105.
Psittacus porphyrocephalus, Shaw, Nat. Misc. pl. 1.
Psittacus euchlorus, Forst. Descr. &c. p. 160.
Psittacus (Psittacula) fringillaceus, Kuhl, Consp. Psitt. pp. 9, 69.
Coriphilus euchlorus, Wagl. Monogr. Psitt. p. 564.
Brotogeris fringillaceus, Steph. Gen. Zool. xiv. p. 133.
Coriphilus pipilans, G. R. Gray, Gen. of B. ii. p. 417.
Coriphilus fringillaceus, Pr. B. Rev. et Mag. de Zool. 1854, p.157.
Lorius fringillaceus, Less. Tr. d'Orn. p. 194.
Brotogeris porphyrocephalus, Swains. Classif. of B. ii. p. 303.
Levaill. Perr. t. 71 ; Ellis's Icon. ined. 13.
' Kohaéngä' of the natives of the Tonga Islands.

Tonga Islands (Tongatabu) ; Sandwich Islands ; Samoan or Navigators' Islands.

TRICHOGLOSSUS MASSENÆ. B.M.

Trichoglossus Massena, Pr. B. Rev. et Mag. de Zool. 1854, p. 157.

New Hebrides (Erromango) ; Solomon Islands.

TRICHOGLOSSUS (?) PALMARUM.

Palm Parrot, Lath. Gen. Syn. i. p. 253.
Psittacus palmarum, Forst. Descr. &c. p. 259 ; G. Forst. Icon.
ined. 48 ; Gmel. S. N. i. p. 329.
Psittacus (Conurus) palmarum, Kuhl, Consp. Psitt. pp. 8, 51.
Trichoglossus palmarum, Wagl. Monogr. Psitt. p. 546.
Nanodes? palmarum, Steph. Gen. Zool. xix. p. 120.
Loriculus? palmarum, Pr. B. Rev. et Mag. de Zool. 1854, p. 157.
Cyclopsitta? palmarum, Pr. B. Cab. Journ. für Ornith. 1856, p.
Coriphilus palmarum, Pr. B. Compt. Rend. 1855, p. 1111.
' Kattènga' of the natives.

New Hebrides (Tanna).

TRICHOGLOSSUS PYGMÆUS.

Pygmy Parrakeet, Lath. Gen. Syn. i. p. 256.
Psittacus pygmæus, Gmel. S. N. i. p. 330.
Trichoglossus? pygmæus, G. R. Gray, List of Psitt. B.M. p. 65.
Islands of the South Seas ; Society Islands (Otaheite). (*Mus. Vienna.*)

TRICHOGLOSSUS PEREGRINUS.

Peregrine Parrot, Lath. Gen. Syn. Suppl. p. 62.
Psittacus peregrinus, Lath. Ind. Orn. i. p. 105.
Trichoglossus peregrinus, G. R. Gray, Gen. of B. ii. p. 411.
Said to be brought from the Islands of the South Seas.

D

ECLECTUS CEYLONENSIS.

Grand Lory, Lath. Gen. Syn. i. p. 275.
Psittacus ceylonensis, Bodd. Tabl. des Pl. Enl. d'Aubent. p. 3.
Psittacus grandis, Gmel. S. N. i. p. 335 ; Voy. de la Coqu. Zool.
i. p. 342.
Eclectus ceylonensis, G. R. Gray, Gen. of B. ii. p. 418.
New Ireland (Port Praslin).

ECLECTUS POLYCHLOROS.

Green and Red Chinese Parrot, Lath. Gen. Syn. i. p. 278.
Psittacus polychloros, Scop. Del. Fl. et Fauna Insubr. p. 87.
Psittacus magnus, Gmel. S. N. i. p. 344.
Psittacus sinensis, Gmel. S. N. i. p. 337 ; Voy. de la Coqu. Zool.
i. p. 342.
Eclectus polychloros, G. R. Gray, Gen. of B. ii. p. 418.
Polychlorus magnus, Sclater, Proc. Z. S. 1857, p. 226.
New Ireland (Port Praslin).

PSITTACUS (GEOFFROY) HETEROCLITUS.

Psittacus Geoffroyi heteroclitus, Homb. & Jacq. Ann. des Sci. N.
n. s. xvi. p. 319.
Pionus heteroclitus, Homb. & Jacq. Voy. au Pôle Sud, i. p. 103.
t. 25*. f. 1.
Geoffroyus heteroclitus, Pr. B. Rev. et Mag. de Zool. 1854, p. 155.
Pionus cyaniceps, Pucher. Voy. au Pôle Sud, Zool. iii. p. 105.
t. 25*. f. 2.
Solomon Islands.

CACATUA (DUCROPSIUS) DUCROPSII.

Cacatua Ducropsii, Homb. & Jacq. Voy. au Pôle Sud, i. p. 108.
t. 26. f. 1.
Plyctolophus Ducrops, Pr. B. Rev. et Mag. de Zool. 1854, p. 156.
Ducropsius typus, Pr. B. Compt. Rend. 1857, p. 537.
Solomon Islands.

CUCULIDÆ.

Note. —The bird represented by Levaillant in t. 79 of his 'Oiseaux
d'Afrique,' and which has been named
Lanius superbus, Shaw, Gen. Zool. vii. p. 293,
Sparactes ——?, Illiger, Prod. Mamm. p. 219,
Sparactes cristatus, Vieill.,
is evidently made up of a specimen of *Pogonias sulcirostris,* though
this remarkably ingenious bird is said to inhabit some of the South
Sea Islands.

CENTROPUS MILO.   B.M.

Centropus Milo, Gould, Proc. Z. S. 1856, p. 136.
Solomon Islands (Guadalcanar).

CENTROPUS ATERALBUS.

Centropus ateralbus, Less. Voy. Coqu. p. 620. t. 34.
‘ Koudouma ’ of the natives.
New Ireland (Port Praslin).

CENTROPUS VIOLACEUS.

Centropus violaceus, Quoy & Gaim. Voy. de l’Astrol. i. p. 229. t. 19.
New Ireland.

EUDYNAMYS TAHITIUS.

Society Cuckow, Lath. Gen. Syn. i. p. 514.
Cuculus fasciatus, Forst. Descr. &c. p. 160 ; G. Forst. Icon.
ined. 56.
Cuculus tahitius, Gmel. S. N. i. p. 412.
Cuculus taitensis, Lath. Ind. Orn. i. p. 209 ; Sparrm. Mus. Carls.
t. 32.
Eudynamys cuneicauda, Peale, U. S. Expl. Exped. p. 139. pl. 22.
f. 2.
Eudynamys taitensis, G. R. Gray, Gen. of B. ii. p. 464.
Cuculus perlatus, Vieill.
‘ Arèva-Rèva ’ or ‘ Ara wereroa ’ or ‘ Ooea ’ of the natives of the
Society Islands.
‘ Kaevaena ’ of the natives of the Marquesas Islands.
Society Islands (Huaheine, Otaheite, Borabora) ; Feejee Islands ;
Cook’s Islands (Hervey Island) ; Tonga Islands (Tongatabu) ; Mar-
quesas Islands.

CUCULUS (CACOMANTIS) SIMUS.

Cuculus simus, Peale, U. S. Expl. Exped. p. 245. pl. 21. f. 1.
Feejee Islands.

CUCULUS (CACOMANTIS) BRONZINUS.   B.M.

Cuculus (Cacomantis) bronzinus, G. R. Gray, Proc. Z. S. 1859,
p. 164.
New Caledonia (Island of Nu).

COLUMBIDÆ.

PTILONOPUS PURPURATUS.   B.M.

Purple-crowned Pigeon, Lath. Gen. Syn. ii. p. 626.
Columba purpurata, Gmel. S. N. i. p. 784 ; G. Forst. Icon. ined.
140.
Columba Kurukuru, Bonn.
Columba Oopa, Wagl. Isis, 1829, p. 742.
Columba Kurukuru, var. *Taitensis,* Less. Voy. de la Coqu. i. p. 297.
Columba porphyracra, pt., Forst. Descr. &c. p. 167.
Columba porphyrea, Wagl. Syst. Av. Col. sp. 31.
Kurukuru DuPetithouarsii, Voy. de la Vénus, t. 7.

Ptilonopus furcatus, Peale, U. S. Expl. Exped. p. 191. pl. 30.
Ptilonopus Nebouxi, Des Murs.
Kurutreron oopa, Pr. B. Consp. Av. ii. p. 26.
Ptilonopus Oopa, G. R. Gray.
Ptilonopus purpuratus, G. R. Gray, List of Col. B.M. p. 4.
Columba taitensis, Less. Compl. Buff. viii. p. 36.
'Oopa' or 'Oo-oòpa' or 'Oopara' or 'Ouba' of the natives of the Society Islands.

Society Islands (Tahiti or New Cythera, Ulietea, Borabora);
Feejee Islands (Ovolau).

? PTILONOPUS ——— ?

Columba porphyracra, pt., Forst. Descr. &c. p. 167.
Society Islands (Ulietea).

PTILONOPUS MERCIERI.

Kurukuru Mercieri, Des Murs.
Ptilopus Mercieri, Pr. B. Consp. Av. ii. p. 22.
Marquesas Islands (Noukahiva).

PTILONOPUS CHRYSOGASTER.   B.M.

Ptilonopus chrysogaster, G. R. Gray, P. Z. S. 1853, p. 48. pl. 54.
Kurutreron chrysogastra, Pr. B. Consp. Av. ii. p. 26.
Ptilinopus taitensis, Reichenb.
Society Islands (Tahiti); Tonga Islands (Tongatabu); Marquesas Islands.

PTILONOPUS XANTHOGASTER.   B.M.

Columba xanthogaster, Wagl. Syst. Av. Col. sp. 29.
Columba purpurata, ♀, Temm.
Columba diademata, Temm. Pl. Col. 254.
Ptilonopus flavigaster, Sw. Classif. of B. ii. p. 347.
Ptilonopus xanthogaster, G. R. Gray, Gen. of B. ii. p. 466.
Thouarsitreron diademata, Pr. B. Consp. Av. ii. p. 16.
Ladrone or Marian Islands.

PTILONOPUS DU PETITHOUARSII.   B.M.

Columba DuPetithouarsii, Neboux, Rev. Zool. 1840, p. 289.
Ptilonopus Æmilius, Less. Descr. Mam. et Ois. 1847, p. 209.
Ptilonopus DuPetithouarsii, G. R. Gray, Gen. of B. iii. App. p. 23; Voy. au Pòle Sud, i. p. 114. t. 29. f. 1.
Columba kurukuru purpuroleucocephalus, Homb. & Jacq. Ann. des Sci. Nat. xiv. p. 316.
Ptilonopus leucocephalus, G. R. Gray, List of Gall. B.M. p. 2.
Thouarsitreron leucocephala, Pr. B. Consp. Av. ii. p. 16.
'Koukou' of the natives.
Marquesas Islands.

PTILONOPUS MARIÆ.   B.M.

Ptilonopus (de Marie), G. R. Gray, Gen. of B. App. p. 23.
Ptilonopus Perousii, Peale, U. S. Expl. Exped. p. 195. pl. 33.
Ptilonopus Mariæ, Jacq. & Pucher. Voy. au Pôle Sud, i. p. 115.
t. 29. f. 2.
Columba Kurukuru superba, Homb. & Jacq. Ann. des Sci. N. xvi.
p. 316.
Ptilopus Mariæ, Pr. B. Consp. Av. ii. p. 22.
Kurukuru samoensis, Des Murs.
'Manu-ma' of the natives of the Samoan Islands.
Feejee Islands (Ngau) ; Samoan or Navigators' Islands.

PTILONOPUS CORALENSIS.

Ptilonopus coralensis, Peale, U. S. Expl. Exped. p. 190. pl. 32.
Kurutreron coralensis, Pr. B. Consp. Av. ii. p. 26.
Low or Paumotu Islands (Island of Carlshoff, &c.).

PTILONOPUS CHALCURUS.   B.M.

Ptilonopus chalcurus, G. R. Gray.
Cook's Islands (Harvey or Hervey Island).
Very similar to the *Ptilonopus coralensis*, but the front and top
of the head shining greyish-purple.

PTILONOPUS ROSEICAPILLUS.   B.M.

Columba roseicapilla, Less. Tr. d'Orn. p. 472.
Columba purpurata, pt., Wagl. Syst. Av. Col. sp. 30 ; Kittl. Kupf.
Vög. t. 33. f. 2.
Ptilonopus purpureocinctus, G. R. Gray, Proc. Z. S. 1853, p. 48.
pl. 55.
Ptilopus roseicapillus, Pr. B. Consp. Av. ii. p. 21 ?
'Totot' of the natives.
Ladrone or Marian Islands (Guam).

? PTILONOPUS —— ?

Columba purpurata, Temm. Pig. t. 34; Wagl. Syst. Av.Col. sp.30.
Ptilonopus fasciatus, pt., Cass.
Society Islands (Otaheite, Ulietea); Tonga Islands (Tongatabu)(?);
Ladrone or Marian Islands (Guam) (?).

PTILONOPUS FASCIATUS.   B.M.

Ptilonopus fasciatus, Peale, U. S. Expl. Exped. p. 193. pl. 31.
Kurukuru samoensis, Fl. Prév. Zool. de la Vénus, p. 247.
Ptilopus apicalis, Pr. B. Consp. Av. ii. p. 23.
'Manu-tagi' of the natives.
Samoan or Navigators' Islands.

Note.—Peale informs us (Expl. Exp. p. 194) that the natives
distinguish another species under the name of 'Manu-rua,' which is

entirely of a green colour. The specimens were found in Upolu, one of the Samoan Islands ; they were lost, however, in the wreck of the U. S. S. Peacock.

PTILONOPUS CLEMENTINÆ.

Ptilonopus (de Clementine), G. R. Gray, Gen. of B. App. p. 23.
Ptilonopus Clementinæ, Homb. & Jacq.Voy. au Pôle Sud, i. p.117. t. 29. f. 3.
Ptilopus Clementinæ, Pr. B. Consp. Av. ii. p. 22.
Feejee Islands ; Samoan or Navigators' Islands (?).

PTILONOPUS GREYI.   B.M.

Ptilonopus Greyi, G. R. Gray.
Ptilopus purpuratus, Pr. B. Consp. Av. ii. p. 19 (nec Wagl.).
Loyalty Islands ; Isle of Pines ; New Hebrides (Erromango) ; Island of Vanikoro.

PTILONOPUS PORPHYRACRUS.   B.M.

Columba porphyracra, Forst. Descr. &c. p. 167 ; G. Forst. Icon. ined. 141.
Columba purpurata, pt., Lath.
Columba porphyracea, Temm. Linn. Trans. xiii. p. 131.
? *Columba Forsteri*, Desm.
Ptilonopus porphyreus, G. R. Gray, Gen. of B. ii. p. 466.
Ptilopus porphyraceus, Pr. B. Consp. Av. ii. p. 21.
' Kurrikuru ' of the natives of the Tonga Islands.
Feejee Islands (Balaou) ; Tonga Islands (Tongatabu).

Note.—It may be noticed that Latham has described a species under the name of
Tabuan Pigeon, Lath. Hist. viii. p. 77,
Columba tabuensis, Lath. MSS.,
as from Tongatabu, which is probably the same as *Ptilonopus por-phyracrus* (?).

PTILONOPUS VIRIDISSIMUS.

Columba purpurata, var., Temm. Pig. t. 35.
Columba viridissima, Temm. (in Pl. Col.).
Columba porphyrea, pt., Wagl. Syst. Av. Col. sp. 31.
Ptilonopus viridissimus, G. R. Gray, Gen. of B. ii. p. 466.
Ptilopus viridissimus, Pr. B. Consp. Av. ii. p. 20.
Society Islands (Ulietea) ; Tonga Islands (Tongatabu).

PTILONOPUS LUTEOVIRENS.   B.M.

Columba luteovirens, Homb. & Jacq. Ann. des Sci. N. n. s. xvi. p. 315.
Calœnas luteovirens, Hartl.Wiegm. Arch. für Naturg. 1852, p. 134.
Ptilonopus luteovirens, Homb. & Jacq.Voy. au Pôle Sud, i. p.112. t. 12. f. 2.

Chrysaena luteovirens, Pr. B. Consp. Av. ii. p. 28.
Columba flava, G. R. Gray, Gen. of B. ii. p. 470.
Calaenas Gouldii, Reichenb.
Calaenas flava, Reichenb.
Columba Feliciæ, Homb. & Jacq. Ann. des Sci. N. n. s. xvi. p. 316 (juv.).
Ptilonopus Feliciæ, Pucher. Voy. au Pôle Sud, i. p.111. t. 12. f.1.
Omeotreron Feliciæ, Pr. B. Consp. Av. ii. p. 27.

Feejee Islands (Balaou).

PTILONOPUS EUGENIÆ. B.M.

Iotreron Eugeniæ, Gould, Proc. Z. S. 1856, p. 137.
Ptilonopus Eugeniæ, G. R. Gray, List of Colum. B.M. p. 6.

Solomon Island.

? PTILONOPUS SUPERBUS.

Columba superba, Temm. Pig. t. 33.
Ptilonopus superbus, (G. R. Gray) Hartl. Wiegm. Arch. für Naturg. 1852, p. 134.
Lamprotreron superbus, pt., Pr. B. Consp. Av. ii. p. 18.
Gould, B. of Austr. pl. 57.

Society Islands (Otaheite) (?).

PTILONOPUS HOLOSERICEUS. B.M.

Ptilonopus holosericeus, G. R. Gray, Gen. of B. ii. p. 467.
Columba holosericea, Temm. Pig. t. 32.
Lamprotreron holosericeus, Pr. B. Consp. Av. ii. p. 18.
Drepanoptila et *Drepanoptera holosericea*, Pr. B. Compt. Rend. 1856, pp. 834, 948.

Isle of Pines ; Sandwich Islands (?).

Note.—Bougainville speaks of a large Pigeon of great beauty, of a green gold colour, with the neck and belly greyish-white, and a little crest on the head (Voyage, Engl. edit. p. 329). He gives the habitat as New Britain.

TRERON CURVIROSTRA.

Hook-billed Pigeon, Lath. Gen. Syn. ii. p. 632. pl. 59.
Columba curvirostra, Gmel. S. N. i. p. 777.
Columba aromatica, pt., Wagl. Syst. Av. Col. sp. 7.
Osmotreron psittacea, pt., Pr. B. Compt. Rend. 1856, p. 949.

New Hebrides (Tanna).

TRERON TANNENSIS.

Columba xanthura, Forst. Isis, 1829, p. 470 ; Descr. &c. p. 264 ; G. Forst. Icon. ined. 138.
Treron aromatica, pt., G. R. Gray, Gen. of B. ii. p. 467.
Ptilonopus xanthura, G. R. Gray, Gen. of B. App. p. 23.

Columba tannensis, Lath. Orn. ii. p. 600.
Columba currirostra, var. β, Gmel. S. N. i. p. 777.
Columba vernans, pt., Wagl. Syst. Av. Col. sp. 9.
Ptilonopus tannensis, G. R. Gray, Gen. of B. ii. p. 467.
Osmotreron psittacea, pt., Pr. B. Compt. Rend. 1856, p. 949.
Osmotreron tannensis, Pr. B. Consp. Av. ii. p. 14.
' Ponnùas ' of the natives.

New Hebrides (Tanna).

CARPOPHAGA (GLOBICERA) PACIFICA.   B.M.

Ferruginous-vented Pigeon, Lath. Gen. Syn. ii. p. 633.
Columba pacifica, Gmel. S. N. i. p. 777.
Carpophaga pacifica, G. R. Gray, Gen. of B. ii. p. 468.
Nutmeg Pigeon, var. A, pt., Lath. Gen. Syn. ii. p. 637.
Columba ænea, var. β, Gmel. S. N. i. p. 780.
Columba oceanica, Kittl. Kupf. Vög. t. 33. f. 1 ?
Columba globicera, Forst. Descr. &c. p. 166 ; G. Forst. Icon.
ined. 139.
Globicera Sundevalli, Pr. B. Consp. Av. ii. p. 32.
Columba ænea, pt., Wagl. Syst. Av. Col. sp. 15.
' Orooba ya ' or ' Ooroobe ' or ' Oorooba ya ' or ' Aroobee ' of the
natives of the Tonga Islands.

Friendly Islands ; Tongatabu or Amsterdam Island ; Eaoowe or
Middleburgh ; Caroline Islands (Oualan and Mortlock's Island).

CARPOPHAGA (GLOBICERA) MICROCERA.

Globicera microcera, Pr. B. Consp. Av. ii. p. 31.
Carpophaga oceanica, pt., Peale, U. S. Expl. Exped. p. 198.
Carpophaga microcera, Cass. U. S. Expl. Exped. p. 263. pl. 29.
' Lupi ' of the natives of Samoan Islands.

Samoan or Navigators' Islands ; Tonga Islands (Tongatabu) ;
Duke of York's Island.

CARPOPHAGA (GLOBICERA) —— ?   B.M.

Columba globicera, var., Forst. Descr. &c. pp. 167, 256.
Globicera pacifica, Pr. B. Consp. Av. ii. p. 30.
New Hebrides (Tanna, Aneitenm).

CARPOPHAGA (GLOBICERA) TARRALI.

Globicera Tarrali, Pr. B. Consp. Av. ii. p. 31.
Island of Vanikoro.

CARPOPHAGA (GLOBICERA) FORSTERI.

Columba globicera, var. I, Forst. Descr. &c. p. 166.
Columba Forsteri, Wagl. Isis, 1829, p. 739.
Carpophaga Forsteri, G. R. Gray, Gen. of B. App. p. 23.
Globicera Forsteri, Pr. B. Consp. Av. ii. p. 30.
Society Islands (Otaheite).

CARPOPHAGA (GLOBICERA) OCEANICA.

Columba oceanica, Less.Voy. de la Coqu. t. 41; Knip & Prev. t. 24.
Globicera oceanica, Pr. B. Consp. Av. ii. p. 31.
Carpophaga oceanica, G. R. Gray, Gen. of B. ii. p. 468.
'Moulousee' or 'Mouleux' of the natives of the Caroline Islands.
'Cyep' of the natives of the Pelew Islands.
Caroline Islands (Oualan); Palaos or Pelew Islands.

CARPOPHAGA (GLOBICERA) RUBRACERA.   B.M.

Carpophaga rubracera, G. R. Gray.
Globicera rubricera, Pr. B. Consp. Av. ii. p. 31.
Carpophaga lepida, Cass.
New Ireland; Solomon Islands.

CARPOPHAGA (GLOBICERA) WILKESII.

Carpophaga Wilkesii, Peale, U. S. Expl. Exped. p. 203. pl. 25.
Globicera Forsteri, pt., Pr. B. Consp. Av. ii. p. 30.
Society Islands (Otaheite, Aurora).

Note.— Ellis has a representation, in his Icon. ined. 72, of a
Pigeon which seems to have the under surface entirely of a cinereous
colour; and this colour also extends over the under tail-coverts. The
Friendly Islands are given by him as the habitat of this bird.

CARPOPHAGA (GLOBICERA) AURORÆ.

Carpophaga auroræ, Peale, U. S. Expl. Exped. p. 201. pl. 24.
Globicera auroræ, Pr. B. Consp. Av. ii. p. 32.
Society Islands (Aurora or Maitia or Metia Island).

CARPOPHAGA (PHAENORHINA) GOLIATH.   B.M.

Carpophaga (Phaenorhina) goliath, G. R. Gray, Proc. Z. S. 1859,
p. 165. pl. 155.
Isle of Pines.

CARPOPHAGA (SERRISIUS) GALEATA.

Serrisius galeatus, Pr. B. Rev. et Mag. de Zool. 1856, p. 401.t.18.
Marquesas Islands (Noukahiva).

Note.—The *Columba auricularis*, Temm. Pig. t. 20,
Columba Temminckii, Wagl. Syst. Av. Col. sp. 40,
Carpophaga ? auricularis, G. R. Gray, Gen. of B. ii. p. 469,
Craspedoenus auricularis, Reichenb.,
Rhagorhina auricularis, Glog.,

is said to inhabit some of the islands of the Pacific Ocean; and
others have more particularly given the Friendly Islands as the abode
of this bird; but it is only an artificial production of some ingenious bird-preserver.

A "large white Pigeon" is mentioned by Cook in his 3rd Voyage, 2nd edit. iii. p. 119, which used to be observed in the Sandwich Islands.

?CARPOPHAGA (MEGALOPREPIA) PUELLA.

Columba puella, Less. Voy. de la Coqu. Zool. i. p. 711.
Carpophaga puella, G. R. Gray, Gen. of B. ii. p. 468.
Megaloprepia puella, Pr. B. Consp. Av. ii. p. 40.
New Ireland.

CARPOPHAGA (DUCULA) PISTRINARIA.   B.M.

Carpophaga vel *Ducula pistrinaria*, Pr. B. Consp. Av. ii. p. 36.
Solomon Islands.

CARPOPHAGA LATRANS.

Carpophaga latrans, Peale, U. S. Expl. Exped. p. 200. pl. 26.
' Manu-mow ' of the natives.
Feejee Islands.

Note.—A species is referred to as the " Pigeon that barked," in Bougainville's Voy., Engl. edit. p. 330, and as found in New Britain.

CARPOPHAGA (ZONOENAS) PINON.

Columba pinon, Quoy & Gaim. Voy. de l'Uranie, i. p. 118. t. 28.
Carpophaga pinon, Selby, Nat. Libr. v. p. 119.
Carpophaga (Zonoenas) pinon, Reichenb. Syst. Av. p. xxvi.
New Ireland.

CARPOPHAGA (IANTHŒNAS) VITIENSIS.   B.M.

Columba vitiensis, Quoy & Gaim. Voy. de l'Astrol. i. p. 246. t. 28.
Carpophaga vitiensis, G. R. Gray, Gen. of B. ii. p. 469.
Ianthaenas vitiensis, Pr. B. Consp. Av. ii. p. 44.
Feejee Islands.

CARPOPHAGA (IANTHŒNAS) CASTANEICEPS.

Columba castaneiceps, Peale, U. S. Expl. Exped. i. p. 187. pl. 23.
Ianthaenas castaneiceps, Pr. B. Consp. Av. ii. p. 45.
Samoan or Navigators' Islands (Upolu).

CARPOPHAGA (IANTHŒNAS) HYPOINOCHROA.   B.M.

Ianthaenas hypoinochroa, Gould, Proc. Z. S. 1856, p. 136.
Carpophaga (Ianthœnas) hypoinochroa, G. R. Gray, List of Co-lum. B.M. p. 24.
New Caledonia ; Isle of Pines.

Note.—What was the "large deep-blue Pigeon," referred to in Bougainville's Voyage, Engl. edit. p. 247, and also by Lesson in

Voy. de la Coqu. i. p. 299, which used to be observed in the Island of Otaheite, but is now no longer found there?

A species is recorded by Kotzebue in his Reise (iii. p. 113), under the name of *Columba australis* (?), as from Radack or Marshall's Islands.

MACROPYGIA ALBICEPS.

Columba amboinensis, Linn. S. N. i. p. 286.
Macropygia amboinensis, Bl. ; Pr. B. Consp. Av. ii. p. 56.
Columba albiceps, Temm. (Mus. Leyd.).
New Caledonia.

MACROPYGIA CARTERETIA.

Macropygia carteretia, Pr. B. Consp. Av. ii. p. 57.
New Ireland.

MACROPYGIA (TURACŒNA) CRASSIROSTRIS.   B.M.

Turacœna crassirostris, Gould, Proc. Z. S. 1856, p. 136.
Macropygia crassirostris, G. R. Gray, List of Colum. B.M. p. 40.
Solomon Islands (Guadalcanar).

TURTUR —— ?

Columba risoria (?), Less. Tr. d'Orn. p. 473.
Tonga Islands.

TURTUR PREVOSTIANUS.

Turtur prevostianus, Pr. B. Consp. Av. ii. p. 62.
Turtur picta, Mus. Par.
Ladrone or Marian Islands.

TURTUR (STREPTOPELIA) GAIMARDI.

Streptopelia gaimardi, Pr. B. Consp. Av. ii. p. 66.
Columba Dussumierii, pt., Wagl. Syst. Av. Col. 99.
Ladrone or Marian Islands (Guam).

Note.—What is the "Turtle Dove" mentioned by Bougainville (Voy., Engl. edit. p. 329) as found in New Britain?

Temminck and Wagler both record that the under-mentioned bird, viz.—

Columba cristata, Temm. Pig. t. 9,
Peristera cristata, G. R. Gray,
Geotrygon cristata, Pr. B. Consp. Av. ii. p. 70,

is from the Friendly Islands (?) ; but it has since been proved to be a species found only in Jamaica.

CALŒNAS NICOBARICA.

Columba nicobarica, Linn. S. N. i. p. 283.
Columba gallus, Wagl. Syst. Av. Col. sp. 113.
Calœnas nicobarica, G. R. Gray, List of Gen. of B. 1840, p. 59.
Goura nicobarica, Steph. Gen. Zool. xi. i. p. 122.
New Ireland (Port Praslin).

CALŒNAS (―――― ?) ERYTHROPTERA.   B.M.

Garnet-winged Pigeon, Lath. Gen. Syn. ii. p. 624.
Columba erythroptera, Gmel. S. N. i. p. 775.
Columba leucophrys, Forst. Descr. &c. p. 168 ; G. Forst. Icon. ined. 136.
Peristera erythroptera, G. R. Gray, List of Gall. B.M. p. 16.
Calœnas erythroptera, G. R. Gray, List of Colum. B.M. p. 64.
Phlegœnas erythroptera, Pr. B. Consp. Av. ii. p. 89.
Pampusana erythroptera, Pr B. Compt. Rend. 1856, p. 947.
Society Islands (Eimeo, Otaheite) ; Low Islands (Bow Island).

Peristera pectoralis, Peale, U.S. Expl. Exped. p. 205.
Low Islands (Carlshoff).

Var. *Columba erythroptera*, var. β, Gmel. S. N. i. p. 775.
' Ooeirao ' of the natives.
Society Islands (Otaheite).

Var. " *Columba pectoralis*," Ellis's Icon. ined. 71.
' Oo-oo widou ' of the natives.
York Island or Eimeo or Imaio.
Front, eyebrows, and all the body white.

Var. " *Columbe érythroptère à gorge blanche*," Quoy & Gaim. Voy. de l'Uranie, Zool. p. 35.
Ladrone or Marian Islands (Guam).

? CALŒNAS (―――― ?) EIMEENSIS.

Purple-breasted Pigeon, Lath. Gen. Syn. ii. p. 629.
Columba eimeensis, Gmel. S. N. i. p. 784.
Treron eimeensis, G. R. Gray.
Society Islands (Eimeo).

? CALŒNAS (――――?) STAIRI.   B.M.

Calœnas (Phlegœnas) Stairi, G. R. Gray, Proc. Z. S. 1856, p. 6. pl. 115.
Pampusana erythroptera, pt., Pr. B. Compt. Rend. 1856, p. 947.
Samoan or Navigators' Islands.

CALŒNAS (——?) FERRUGINEA.

Garnet-winged Pigeon, var. B, Lath. Gen. Syn. ii. p. 625.
Columba erythroptera, var. γ, Gmel. S. N. i. p. 775.
Phlegœnas erythroptera, pt., Pr. B.
Columba ferruginea, Forst. Descr. &c. p. 265 ; G. Forst. Icon.
ined. 142.
Columba curvirostra, Licht. in Forst. l. c. p. 265, note.
Treron ferruginea, G. R. Gray, Gen. of B. App. p. 23.
Osmotreron fulvicollis, pt., Pr. B. Consp. Av. ii. p. 14.
' Mahk ' of the natives.
New Hebrides (Tanna).

CALŒNAS (PAMPUSANA) RUBESCENS.
Columba rubescens, Vieill. N. Dict. xxvi. p. 346 ; Krusenst. Voy.
t. 17.
Columba pyrrhacra, Forst. Descr. &c. p. 211 ?
Pampusana rubescens, Pr. B. Consp. Av. ii. p. 90.
Phlegœnas erythroptera, pt., Pr. B. Compt. Rend. 1856, p. 949.
Marquesas Islands (Noukahiva).

CALŒNAS (PAMPUSANA) XANTHURA.
Columba pampusan, Quoy & Gaim. Voy. l'Uranie, p. 121. t. 30.
Pampusana xanthura, (Cuv.) Pr. B. Consp. Av. ii. p. 89.
Peristera erythroptera, (Gm.) Cass. U. S. Expl. Exped. 1858,
p. 277.
Pampusana erythroptera, pt., Pr. B. Compt. Rend. 1856, p. 947.
Ladrone or Marian Islands (Guam).

CALŒNAS (PAMPUSANA) ROUSSEAU.
Columba xanthonura, Temm. Pl. Col. 190.
Pampusana rousseau, Pr. B. Consp. Av. ii. p. 89.
Columba pampusan, pt., Wagl. Syst. Av. Col. sp. 82.
Phlegœnas erythroptera, pt., Pr. B. Compt. Rend. 1856, p. 949.
" Ins. Marchion."

? CALŒNAS (—— ?) ——?
Pacific Pigeon, Lath. Hist. of B. viii. p. 45.
Tonga Islands (Mayorga or Vavao or Vavau or Howe's Island).

CHALCOPHAPS CHRYSOCHLORA.   B.M.
Chalcophaps chrysochlora, var., G. R. Gray, P. Z. S. 1859, p. 165.
' Maak ' of the natives.
New Hebrides (Tanna) ; New Caledonia (Island of Nu).

CHALCOPHAPS STEPHANI.
Peristera Stephani, Homb. & Jacq. Voy. au Pôle Sud, i. p. 119.
t. 28. f. 2.
Chalcophaps Stephani, Reichenb.
Solomon Islands (St. George).

GOURA CORONATA.

Columba coronata, Linn. S. N. i. p. 282.
Goura coronata, Steph. Gen. Zool. xi. i. p. 120.
Lophyrus indicus, Steph. Gen. Zool. xiv. p. 294. pl. 19.
" *Crown Bird,*" Bougainv. Voyage, Engl. edit. p. 329.
New Britain ; New Ireland.

DIDUNCULUS STRIGIROSTRIS.

Gnathodon strigirostris, Jard. Ann. Nat. Hist. 1845, xvi. p. 175.
pl. 9.
   Didunculus strigirostris, Peale, U. S. Expl. Exped. p. 209. pl. 34.
Pleiodus strigirostris, Reichenb.
Gould, B. of Austr. pl. 76 ; G. R. Gray and Mitch. Gen. of B. ii.
pl. 120*.
   ' Manu-mea ' of the natives.
Samoan or Navigators' Islands (Upolu).   (*Mus. Jardine.*)

MEGAPODIDÆ.

MEGAPODIUS LA PEROUSII.

Megapodius La Perousii, Quoy & Gaim. Voy. l'Uranie, p. 127. t. 33.
' Sassegniat ' of the natives.
Ladrone or Marian Islands (Tinian).

MEGAPODIUS —— ?   B.M.

The egg only of a *Megapodius* has been brought from the Samoan or Navigators' Islands ; but no example of the perfect bird has yet been recorded by naturalists or others as from that locality.

MEGAPODIUS —— ?   B.M.

The egg only of a *Megapodius* has also been obtained from the Hapace Islands ; but the perfect bird is unknown to naturalists.

PHASIANIDÆ.

GALLUS BANKIVA, var.

Gallus Bankiva, var., G. R. Gray.
Gallus bankiva, var. *tahiticus,* Peale, U.S. Expl. Exped. p. 180. fig.
Society, Tonga, Feejee, and Sandwich Islands, New Caledonia, &c.

STRUTHIONIDÆ.

CASUARIUS BENNETTII.   B.M.

Casuarius Bennettii, Gould, Proc. Z. S. 1857, p. 268. pl. 129 ;
Benn. Proc. Z. S. 1859, p. 32.
   ' Mooruk ' of the natives.
New Britain.

CHARADRIADÆ.

CHARADRIUS FULVUS. B.M.

Fulvous Plover, Lath. Gen. Syn. iii. p. 211.
Charadrius fulvus, Gmel. S. N. i. p. 687.
Charadrius glaucopus, Forst. Descr. &c. p. 176.
Charadrius taitensis, Less. Man. d'Ornith. ii. p. 321.
Pluvialis fulvus, Pr. B. Compt. Rend. 1856, p. 417.
Charadrius pluvialis, pt., Gmel. S. N. i. p. 688.
Charadrius pluvialis, Peale, U. S. Expl. Exped. p. 239.
Charadrius xanthocheilus, (Wagl.) Gould, B. of Austr. vi. pl. 13 ;
Cass. U. S. Expl. Exped. 1858, p. 325.
Charadrius virginianus, (Bonap.) Hartl. Wiegm. Arch. für Naturg.
1852, p. 134.
Pluvialis xanthocheilus, Pr. B. Compt. Rend. 1856, p. 417.
Pluvialis longipes, pt., Pr. B. Compt. Rend. 1855, p. 417.
G. Forst. Icon. ined. 123 ; Ellis's Icon. ined. 68.
'Turi' of the natives of the Marquesas Islands.

Society Islands (Otaheite) ; Low or Paumotu Islands (Bow Island,
&c.) ; Marquesas Islands ; York Island ; Sandwich Islands (Oahu) ;
Christmas Island ; New Hebrides ; Samoan or Navigators', Feejee,
and Tonga Islands.

Var. ? *Charadrius glaucopus*, var., Forst. Descr. &c. p. 258 ; G.
Forst. Icon. ined. 124.
Charadrius ——?, G. R. Gray, Proc. Z. S. 1859, p. 165.
'Poemanghee' of the natives.
New Caledonia.

CHARADRIUS LONGIPES?

Charadrius pluvialis, (L.) Horsf. Linn. Trans. xiii. p. 187.
Charadrius longipes, Temm.
Charadrius orientalis, Schleg.
Charadrius virginicus, Blyth, Cat. of B. p. 262.
Charadrius virginianus, pt., Hartl. Wiegm. Arch. für Naturg.
1852, p. 134.
Pluvialis longipes, Pr. B. Compt. Rend. 1856, p. 417.

Ladrone or Marian Islands ; Caroline Islands (Oualan) ; Gilbert's
Islands (Kingsmill Islands)?

CHARADRIUS ——?

Ringed Plover, var. A, pt., Lath. Gen. Syn. iii. p. 203.
Charadrius Hiaticula, var. β, pt., Gmel. S. N. i. p. 683.
Sandwich Islands (Owhyhee).

Note.—Latham has recorded the Friendly Islands as a habitat
for the following bird :—

White Sheathbill, Lath. Gen. Syn. iii. p. 268. pl. 89,
Chionis alba, Forst.,
Vaginalis alba, Gmel. S. N. i. p. 705 ;

but this is concluded to be a mistake, as the specimens are usually brought from the Straits of Magellan.

CINCLUS INTERPRES.   B.M.

Tringa interpres, Linn. S. N. i. p. 248.
Strepsilas interpres, Leach, Cat. of Brit. Birds, p. 29.
Strepsilas collaris, Temm. Man. d'Orn. ii. p. 553.
Tringa Oahuensis, Bloxh. Byron's Voy. p. 251.
Strepsilas melanocephala, Pr. B.
Gould, B. of Austr. vi. pl. 39.
'Toria' of the natives of the Sandwich Islands.

New Hebrides (Aneiteum); New Caledonia; Sandwich Islands; Ladrone or Marian Islands; Gilbert's Islands (Kingsmill Group). Many of the islands north and south of the Equator (*Peale*).

ARDEIDÆ.

ARDEA (HERODIAS) SACRA.   B.M.

Blue Heron, pt., Lath. Gen. Syn. iii. p. 78.
Ardea cærulea, pt., Gmel. S. N. i. p. 631.
Ardea jugularis, Forst. Descr. &c. p. 172.
Herodias jugularis, Gould, B. of Austr. vii. pl. 60.
Ardea novæ hollandiæ, (Lath.) Licht.
Ardea Matook, Vieill.; G. Forst. Icon. ined. 114 ?
Sacred Heron, Lath. Gen. Syn. iii. p. 92.
Ardea sacra, Gmel. S. N. i. p. 640.
Ardea æquinoctialis, (nec Gm.) Forst. Descr. &c. p. 156.
Herodias Greyi, G. R. Gray, List of Gall. &c. B.M. p. 80; Gould, B. of Austr. vii. pl. 61.
Herodias sacra, Pr. B. Consp. Av. ii. p. 121.
'Otai' of the natives of the Society Islands.
'Matuku' of the natives of the Marquesas Islands.
'Otoo' of the natives of the Sandwich Islands.

Society, Low, Cook's, Sandwich, and Marquesas Islands; New Caledonia.

ARDEA (HERODIAS) ALBOLINEATA.   B.M.

Ardea (Herodias) albolineata, G. R. Gray, Proc. Z. S. 1859, p.166.
Herodius pannosa, Gould, B. of Austr. vi. pl. 59 ?
Ellis's Icon. ined. 58 ? (white state).

Isle of Pines; Feejee Islands (Matuku); Tonga? and Samoan? Islands.

ARDEA (HERODIAS) ATRA.

Ardea atra, Cuv. (nec Gm.).
Ardea jugularis, Less. Tr. d'Orn. p. 575.
Herodias atra, Pr. B. Consp. Av. ii. p. 121.

Ladrone or Marian Islands; Caroline Islands (Oualan)?

ARDEA (BUTORIDES) STAGNALIS.

Ardea stagnalis, (Gould) Cass. U. S. Expl. Exped. 1858, p. 297.
Ardea patruelis, Peale, U. S. Expl. Exped. p. 216.
Butorides patruelis, Pr. B. Consp. Av. ii. p. 130.
Gould, B. of Austr. vi. pl. 67.
Society Islands (Otaheite).

ARDEA (ARDETTA) EXILIS.

Ardea exilis, Peale, U. S. Expl. Exped. p. 216.
Botaurus exilis?, Cass. U. S. Expl. Exped. p. 300.
Ardea pusilla, Vieill. ?
Ardetta pusilla, Gould, B. of Austr. vii. pl. 68.
Society Islands (Oahu).

ARDEA (ARDETTA) SINENSIS.

Ardea sinensis, Gmel. S. N. i. p. 642 ?
"*Petit Héron aux ailes noires,*" Quoy & Gaim. Voy. de l'Uranie,
Zool. i. p. 536.
Ardea lepida, (Horsf.) Less. Tr. d'Orn. p. 573.
'Kakag' of the natives.
Ladrone or Marian Islands.

NYCTICORAX CALEDONICUS.

Caledonian Night Heron, Lath. Gen. Syn. iii. p. 55.
Ardea ferruginea, Forst. Descr. &c. p. 274 ; G. Forst. Icon. ined.
111.
Ardea caledonica, Gmel. S. N. i. p. 626.
Ardea Sparmanni, Wagl. Syst. Av. Ard. sp. 32.
Nycticorax caledonicus, Steph. Gen. Zool. xi. p. 613.
Gould, B. of Austr. vi. pl. 63.
New Caledonia.

Note.—The *A. caledonica,* juv., figured by Kittlitz in his Kupf.
Vög. t. 35. f. 2, is the young of *N. crassirostris,* Vigors.

NYCTICORAX MANILLENSIS (?).

Nycticorax manillensis, juv., Pr. B. Consp. Av. ii. p. 140.
Solomon Islands.

(?) NYCTICORAX OCEANICUS.

Nycticorax oceanicus, Less. ; Hartl. Wiegm. Arch. für Naturg.
1852, p. 135.
Marquesas Islands.

SCOLOPACIDÆ.

NUMENIUS TAHITIENSIS.

Scolopax phaeopus, Linn. An. ? ; Forst. Descr. &c. p. 242 ; G.
Forst. Icon. ined. 131.

E

Otaheite Curlew, Lath. Gen. Syn. iii. p. 122.
Scolopax tahitiensis, Gmel. S. N. i. p. 656.
Numenius tahitiensis, Lath. Ind. Orn. ii. p. 711.
Scolopax arquata, pt., Gmel. S. N. i. p. 655?
'Tevrea' or 'Tewèa' or 'Tewèh' of the natives of the Society Islands.
'Torata' of the natives of the Sandwich Islands.

Society Islands (Otaheite); Cook's Islands (Harvey Island, Ota-kootaia or Waneoaette) ; New Caledonia ; Sandwich Islands ; Christmas Island.

NUMENIUS FEMORALIS.

Numenius femoralis, Peale, U. S. Expl. Exped. p. 233. pl. 37.

Low or Paumotu Islands (Vincennes Island or Kawake).

NUMENIUS ——?

"*Corlieux*," Quoy & Gaim. Voy. de l'Uranie, i. p. 35.

Ladrone or Marian Islands ; Gilbert's Islands (Kingsmill Islands?).

LIMOSA NOVÆ ZEALANDIÆ.   B.M.

Limosa novæ zealandiæ, G. R. Gray, Voy. Ereb. & Terr. Birds, p. 13; Cass. U. S. Expl. Exped. 1858, p. 314.
Limosa Foxii, Peale, U. S. Expl. Exped. p. 231.
Limosa hudsonica, var. *a*, Pr. B. Compt. Rend. 1856, p. 597.

Samoan or Navigators' Islands (Rose Island) ; New Hebrides (Aneiteum).

TOTANUS (GAMBETTA) INCANUS.   B.M.

Ash-coloured Snipe, Lath. Gen. Syn. iii. p. 154.
Scolopax incana, Gmel. S. N. i. p. 658.
Totanus incanus, Vieill. N. Dict. d'Hist. Nat. vi. p. 400.
Scolopax solitarius, Bloxh. Byron's Voy. p. 252.
Totanus oceanicus, Less. Compl. Buff. p. 244.
Scolopax undulata, Forst. Descr. &c. p. 173.
Scolopax pacifica, Forst. Descr. &c. p. 174.
Totanus polynesiæ, Peale, U. S. Expl. Exped. p. 237.
Totanus pacificus, Hartl. Wiegm. Arch. für Naturg. 1852, p. 134.
Totanus solitaris, Hartl. Wiegm. Arch. für Naturg. 1852, p. 135.
Gambetta oceanica, Pr. B. Compt. Rend. 1856, p. 597.
'Toria' or 'Torea' of the natives of the Society Islands.
'Kivi' of the natives of the Marquesas Islands.

Society, Low, Marquesas, Sandwich, Tonga, Feejee, and Samoan Islands; Palmerston Island, &c.

Differs from the Australian and Japanese birds in the nasal groove being more than half the length of the bill.

TOTANUS BREVIPES.

Totanus brevipes, Vieill. N. Dict. d'Hist. Nat. vi. p. 410.
Totanus pedestris, Less. Tr. d'Orn. p. 582.
" *Chevalier bécasseaux,*" Less. & Garn. Voy. de la Coqu. Zool. i.
p. 432?
Ladrone or Marian Islands ; Caroline Islands (Oualan)?

TOTANUS (TRINGOIDES) HYPOLEUCUS.

Totanus hypoleucus, (Temm.) Less. Tr. d'Orn. p. 552.
Actitis empusa, Gould, B. of Austr. vii. pl. 35.
Ladrone or Marian Islands.

TOTANUS (TRYNGITES?) CANCELLATUS.

Barred Phalarope, Lath. Gen. Syn. iii. p. 274.
Tringa cancellata, Gmel. S. N. i. p. 675 ; Ellis's Icon. ined. 64.
Phalaropus cancellatus, Lath. Ind. Orn. ii. p. 777.
Tringa parvirostris, Peale, U. S. Expl. Exped. p. 235. pl. 38. f. 1.
Actiturus rufescens, (Vieill.) var. *b,* Pr. B. Compt. Rend. 1856,
p. 597.
Christmas Island ; Low or Paumotu Islands (Honden or Houden
or Dog? and Raraka Island) ; Cook's Islands (Hervey Island)?

TRINGA (PROSOBONIA) LEUCOPTERA.

White-winged Sandpiper, Lath. Gen. Syn. iii. p. 172. pl. 82.
Tringa pyrrhetraea, Forst. Descr. &c. p. 174 ; G. Forst. Icon.
ined. 120 ; Ellis's Icon. ined. 65.
Tringa leucoptera, Gmel. S. N. i. p. 678.
Totanus leucopterus, Vieill. N. Dict. d'Hist. Nat. vi. p. 396.
Prosobonia leucoptera, Pr. B. Compt. Rend. 1856, p. 598.
' Torowe ' of the natives of Otaheite.
' Teetee ' or ' Tete ' of the natives of Eimeo.
Society Islands (Otaheite ; Eimeo or York Island).

RALLIDÆ.

RALLUS PACIFICUS.

Pacific Rail, Lath. Gen. Syn. iii. p. 235.
Rallus pacificus, Forst. Descr. &c. p. 177 ; G. Forst. Icon. ined.
128 ; Gmel. S. N. i. p. 717.
' Oomnaa ' or ' Eboonàa ' of the natives of the Society Islands.
' Oomeia-Keteòw ' of the natives of the Tonga Islands.
Society Islands (Otaheite) ; Tonga Islands (Tongatabu).

RALLUS PHILIPPENSIS?

Rallus philippensis, Linn. S. N. i. p. 263.
Hypotænidia philippensis, Pr. B. Compt. Rend. 1856, p. 599.
" *Râle tiklin,*" Quoy & Gaim. Voy. de l'Uranie, Zool. i. p. 35.
Ladrone or Marian Islands.

RALLUS PECTORALIS.   B.M.

Rallus pectoralis, Cuv., Less. Tr. d'Orn. p. 536 ; Cass. U. S. Expl.
Exped. 1858, p. 303 ; Gould, B. of Austr. vi. pl. 76.
Rallus philippensis, (Lath.) Peale, U. S. Expl. Exped. p. 222 ;
Hartl. Wiegm. Arch. für Naturg. 1852, p. 136.
Philippine Rail, var. A, Lath. Gen. Syn. iii. p. 231. pl. 86.
Rallus philippensis, var. β, Gmel. S. N. i. p. 714.
Rallus pacificus, var., Forst. Descr. &c. p. 178 ; G. Forst. Icon.
ined. 127.
Rallus Forsteri, Hartl. Wiegm. Arch. für Naturg. 1852, p. 136.
' Namoka ' of the natives of the Tonga Islands.

Society Islands (Otaheite); Samoan or Navigators' Islands(Upolu);
Feejee Islands (Mathuata) ; Tonga Islands (Tongatabu).

Var. ? *Philippine Rail,* var. B, Lath. Gen. Syn. v. p. 232.
Rallus philippensis, var. δ, Gmel. S. N. i. p. 714.
Tonga Islands (Tongatabu).

ORTYGOMETRA ? SANDWICHENSIS.

Sandwich Rail, Lath. Gen. Syn. iii. p. 236.
Rallus ecaudatus, Cook's 3rd Voy. 2nd edit. iii. p. 119.
Rallus sandwichensis, Gmel. S. N. i. p. 717 ; Ellis's Icon. ined.
70 (?).
Porzana sandwichensis, Hartl. Wiegm. Arch. für Naturg. 1852,
p. 137.
Corethrura sandwichensis, G. R. Gray, Gen. of B. iii. p. 595.
Zapornia sandwichensis, Reichenb. Syst. Av. t. . f. 1184, 1185 ?
Sandwich Islands.

ORTYGOMETRA ──— ?

Rallus sandwichensis, var. β, Gmel. S. N. i. p. 717.
New Hebrides (Tanna).

ORTYGOMETRA TANNENSIS.   B.M.

Rallus tannensis, Forst. Descr. &c. p. 275 ; G. Forst. Icon. ined.
131.
Rallus quadristrigatus, Horsf. Linn. Trans. xiii. p. 196.
Gallinula mystacina, Temm.
Porzana leucophrys, Gould, B. of Austr. vi. pl. 81.
Corethrura tannensis, G. R. Gray, Gen. of B. iii. p. 595.
New Hebrides (Tanna) ; Feejee Islands (Ngau).

ORTYGOMETRA TAHITIENSIS.

Otaheite Rail, Lath. Gen. Syn. iii. p. 236.
Rallus tahitiensis, Gmel. S. N. i. p. 717.
Corethrura tahitiensis, G. R. Gray, Gen. of B. iii. p. 595.
Porzana tahitiensis, Hartl. Wiegm. Arch. für Naturg. 1852, p.136.
Zapornia? tahitiensis, Pr. B. Compt. Rend. 1856, p. 599.
Society Islands (Otaheite) ; Friendly Islands.

ORTYGOMETRA OBSCURA.

Dusky Rail, Lath. Gen. Syn. iii. p. 237.
Rallus obscurus, Gmel. S. N. i. p. 718.
Corethrura obscura, G. R. Gray, Gen. of B. iii. p. 595.
Porzana obscura, Hartl. Wiegm. Arch. für Naturg. 1852, p. 137.
Sandwich Islands.

ORTYGOMETRA TABUENSIS.   B.M.

Tabuan Rail, Lath. Gen. Syn. iii. p. 235.
Rallus minutus, Forst. Descr. &c. p. 178; G. Forst. Icon. ined. 130.
Rallus tabuensis, Gmel. S. N. i. p. 717.
Ortygometra tabuensis, G. R. Gray, Voy. Ereb. & Terr. Birds, p. 14.
Porzana tabuensis, Hartl. Wiegm. Arch. für Naturg. 1852, p. 136.
Zapornia? tabuensis, Pr. B. Compt. Rend. 1856, p. 599.
Gallinula immaculata, Swains. Two and a Quarter Cent. p. 377.
Porzana? immaculata, Gould, B. of Austr. vi. pl. 82.
Zapornia spilonota, (Gould) Peale, U. S. Expl. Exped. p. 224.
Zapornia umbrina, Cass. Proc. Ac. Philad. 1856, viii. p. 254.
Zapornia umbrata, Hartl. Wiegm. Arch. für Naturg. 1858, ii.
p. 29.
Porzana spilonota, Hartl. Wiegm. Arch. für Naturg. 1852, p. 136.
Crex plumbea, Gray, Griff. Anim. Kingd. iii. p. 400.
Corethrura tabuensis, G. R. Gray, Gen. of B. iii. p. 595, App. 27.
' Mœho ' of the natives of the Society Islands.
' Nŏhur ' of the natives of New Hebrides.

Society Islands (Otaheite) ; Tonga Islands (Tongatabu) ; Feejee
Islands (Ngau, Ovolau) ; New Hebrides (Tanna, Aneiteum).

PORPHYRIO SAMOENSIS.   B.M.

Porphyrio indicus, (Horsf.) Cass. U. S. Expl. Exped. 1858, p. 308.
Porphyrio samoensis, Peale, U. S. Expl. Exped. p. 220.
Samoan or Navigators' Islands (Upolu).

PORPHYRIO VITIENSIS.   B.M.

Porphyrio vitiensis, Peale, U. S. Expl. Exped. p. 221.
Porphyrio poliocephalus, (Lath.) ? Pr. B. Compt. Rend. 1856,
p. 599.
Porphyrio pulverulentus, (Temm.) G. R. Gray, List of Ans. B.M.
p. 121 (young bird).
Fulica porphyrio, Forst. Descr. &c. p. 156 ?

Feejee Islands (Viti Levu) ; Tonga Islands (Tongatabu)? ; New
Hebrides (Tanna)? ; New Caledonia ?

GALLINULA ——?

Gallinula tenebrosa, Gould ? ; Ellis's Icon. ined. 69.
Fulica chloropus, (L.) Bloxh. Byron's Voy. p. 250.
' Alai ' of the natives.
Sandwich Islands.

GALLINULA —— ?

" *Poule d'eau*," Quoy & Gaim. Voy. de l'Uranie, Zool. i. p. 35.
Gallinula orientalis, Horsf. ?

Ladrone or Marian Islands.

FULICA ALAI.

Fulica atra, (L.) Bloxh. Byron's Voy. p. 251.
Fulica alai, Peale, U. S. Expl. Exped. p. 224. pl. 36.

Sandwich Islands.

ANATIDÆ.

BERNICLA SANDWICHENSIS.   B.M.

Bernicla sandwichensis, Vigors; Jard. & Selby, Orn. Illustr. n. s.
pl. 8.
Anser hawaiensis, Eyd. & Soul. Voy. Bonite, t. 10.
' Na-na ' of the natives?

Sandwich Islands (Owhyhee).

DENDROCYGNA VAGANS.   B.M.

Dendrocygna vagans, Eyton, MSS.
Morillon des îles Mariannes, Less. Tr. d'Orn. p. 632?
Dendrocygna arcuata, (Cuv.) Gould, B. of Austr. vii. pl. 14.
Dendrocygna arcuata, var. *c*, *Gouldi*, Pr. B. Compt. Rend. 1856,
p. 649.

Feejee Islands (Viti Levu) ; Ladrone or Marian Islands?

This bird differs from the *D. arcuata*, Cuv., in having black and
white upper tail-coverts, &c.   The Feejee and Manilla birds are
smaller than those found on the continent of India.

Note.—Wild Geese and Ducks of a small size frequent the [Sand-
wich] islands in the winter season, most probably from the north-
west coast of America.—*Bloxh., Byron's Voy.* p. 251.

ANAS BOSCHAS (?).

"*Anas boschas*, ? L.," Hartl. Wiegm. Arch. für Naturg. 1852,
p. 122.

Sandwich Islands (Oahu).

Note.—Muscovy Ducks are stated to be found at Ovolau, one of
the Feejee Islands.

ANAS SUPERCILIOSA, var.

Supercilious Duck, Lath. Gen. Syn. iii. p. 497.
? *Anas superciliosa*, Gmel. S. N. i. p. 537.
? *Anas leucophrys*, Forst. Descr. &c. p. 93; G. Forst. Icon. ined. 77.
Anas superciliosa, var. *Sandwichensis*, Pr. B. Compt. Rend. 1856,
p. 649.
' Mora ' of the natives of the Society Islands.

New Caledonia ; Samoan or Navigators' Islands (Upolu); Tonga

Islands (Tongatabu); Feejee Islands; Society Islands (Otaheite);
Sandwich Islands.

ANAS PUNCTATA, var.

Anas punctata, (Gould?); var. G. R. Gray, Proc. Z. S. 1859, p. 166.
New Caledonia.

CHAULELASMUS STREPERA, var. (?)

Anas strepera, var., Forst.; Hartl. Wiegm. Arch. für Naturg. 1852,
p. 136.
Society Islands; New Caledonia.

SPATULA CLYPEATA (?).

Anas clypeata, Linn.; Peale, U. S. Expl. Exped. p. 251.
Sandwich Islands (Oahu; Owhyhee).

PROCELLARIDÆ.

PUFFINUS PACIFICUS.

Pacific Petrel, Lath. Gen. Syn. iii. p. 416.
Procellaria pacifica, Gmel. S. N. i. p. 560.
Nectris fuliginosus, (Sol.) Banks's Icon. ined. 23*.
Procellaria fuliginosa, Kuhl, Monogr. sp. 27.
Puffinus pacificus, G. R. Gray, Gen. of B. iii. p. 647.
Euopoa and other islands of the Pacific Seas.

PUFFINUS OBSCURUS.

Dusky Petrel, Lath. Gen. Syn. iii. p. 416.
Procellaria obscura, Gmel. S. N. i. p. 559.
Puffinus assimilis, Gould, B. of Austr. vii. pl. 59.
Puffinus obscurus, Vieill. Gal. des Ois. t. 301 ?
Cimotomus obscurus, Macgill. ?
Christmas Island.

PROCELLARIA GIGANTEA.

Procellaria gigantea, Gmel. S. N. i. p. 563.
Procellaria ossifraga, Forst. Descr. &c. p. 343; Icon. ined. 93[a].
Ossifraga gigantea, Reichenb.
Gould, B. of Austr. vii. pl. 45.
Christmas Island.

PROCELLARIA (AESTRELATA) DESOLATA.

Brown-banded Petrel, Lath. Gen. Syn. iii. p. 409.
Procellaria desolata, Gmel. S. N. i. p. 562.
Procellaria fasciata, Bonn.
Aestrelata desolata, Pr. B. Consp. Av. ii. p. 189.
Ellis, Icon. ined. 43.
Caroline Islands.

* A series of drawings made by Sydney Parkinson during Cook's first Voyage
in the years 1768 to 1771, but usually referred to as above. They are in the
Banksian Collection of the British Museum.

PROCELLARIA (AESTRELATA) ROSTRATA.

Procellaria rostrata, Peale, U. S. Expl. Exped. p. 296. pl. 41.
Aestrelata desolata, var. *a*, Pr. B. Consp. Av. ii. p. 189.
Society Islands (Otaheite).

PROCELLARIA (AESTRELATA) ALBA.

White-breasted Petrel, Lath. Gen. Syn. iii. p. 400.
Procellaria alba, Gmel. S. N. i. p. 565 ; Bloxh. Byron's Voy.
p. 252.
Procellaria variegata, Bonn.
Aestrelata leucocephala?, Pr. B. Consp. Av. ii. p. 189.
' Uau ' of the natives of the Sandwich Islands.
Turtle and Christmas Isles ; Sandwich Islands.

PROCELLARIA (——?) PARVIROSTRIS.

Procellaria parvirostris, Peale, U. S. Expl. Exped. p. 298. pl. 40.
Low or Paumotu Islands (Honden Island).

PROCELLARIA GAVIA.

Procellaria gavia, Forst. Descr. &c. pp. 148, 156.
New Caledonia.

PROCELLARIA (DAPTION) CAPENSIS.

Procellaria capensis, Linn.
Daption capensis, Steph.
Forst. Icon. ined. 96 ; Gould, B. of Austr. vii. pl. 53.
' Koputu ' of the natives.
Marquesas Islands.

THALASSIDROMA (BULWERIA) MACGILLIVRAYI.   B.M.

Like *T. Bulweri*, but with the bill rather larger; and it is without
the sooty-brown on the wings.
Feejee Islands (Ngau).

THALASSIDROMA (FREGETTA) MELANOGASTER.

Procellaria Fregata, Forst. Descr. &c. p. 180 ; Icon. ined. 13?, 14.
Procellaria grallaria, Licht.
Thalassidroma oceanica, Pr. B.
Thalassidroma melanogaster, Gould, B. of Austr. viii. pl. 65.
Fregetta melanogastra, Pr. B. Consp. Av. ii. p. 198.
Society Islands (Otaheite).

THALASSIDROMA (FREGETTA) TROPICA.

Thalassidroma tropica, Gould, Ann. & Mag. Nat. Hist. 1844, xiii.
p. 366.
Fregetta tropica, Pr. B. Consp. Av. ii. p. 197.
Thalassidroma leucogaster, Gould, B. of Austr. vii pl. 63.
Banks's Icon. ined. 14.
' Pitau ' of the natives.
Marquesas Islands.

THALASSIDROMA FULIGINOSA.

Sooty Petrel, Lath. Gen. Syn. iii. p. 409.
Procellaria fuliginosa, Gmel. S. N. i. p. 562.
Thalassidroma melania ?, Pr. B. Consp. Av. ii. p. 196.
Thalassidroma fuliginosa, G. R. Gray, Gen. of B. iii. p. 648.
Society Islands (Otaheite) ; Low or Paumotu Islands (Honden Island).

THALASSIDROMA FASCIOLATA.

Thalassidroma fasciolata, Tschudi, Cab. Journ. Orn. 1856, p. 180.
Aurora Island.

THALASSIDROMA (OCEANITES) LINEATA.

Thalassidroma lineata, Peale, U. S. Expl. Exped. p. 293. pl. 39.
Oceanites lineata, Pr. B. Consp. Av. ii. p. 200.
Feejee Islands (Upolu).

DIOMEDEA EXULANS.

Diomedea exulans, Linn. S. N. i. p. 214.
Gould, B. of Austr. vii. pl. 38.
Forst. Icon. ined. 99.
Marquesas Islands.

DIOMEDEA FULIGINOSA.

Diomedea fuliginosa, Gmel. S. N. i. p. 568; Forst. Icon. ined.102 ;
Gould, B. of Austr. vii. t. 44.
Diomedea antarctica, Banks's Icon. ined. 26.
Diomedea palpebrata, Forst. Descr. &c. p. 55 ; Icon. ined. 102.
Phoebetria fuliginosa, Reichenb.
Marquesas Islands.

DIOMEDEA —— ?

"*Albatross,*" Quoy & Gaim. Voy. de l'Uranie, Zool. p. 145.
Between the Ladrone or Marian Islands and Sandwich Islands.

LARIDÆ.

LESTRIS HARDYI.

Lestris hardyi, Pr. B. Compt. Rend. 1856, p. 20.
Between the Philippine and Sandwich Islands.

LARUS (BRUCHIGAVIA) POMARE.

Larus pomare, Bruch, Cab. Journ. Orn. 1853, p. 103 ; Hartl.
Wiegm. Arch. für Naturg. 1852, p. 137.
Gavia pomare, Bruch.
Bruchigavia pomare, Pr. B. Consp. Av. ii. p. 229.
Gelastes Pomare, Pr. B. Compt. Rend. 1856, p. 771.
Society Islands (Otaheite) ; Marquesas Islands.

LARUS (BRUCHIGAVIA) JAMESONI.

Crimson-bill Gull, Lath. Hist. x. p. 145.
Larus canus, Anders.
Larus scopulinus, Forst. Descr. &c. p. 257 ; G. Forst. Icon. ined.
109 (very young).
Larus novæ hollandiæ, Steph.
Larus Jamesonii, Wils. Ill. of Zool. pl.
Xema Jamesoni, Gould, B. of Austr. vii. pl. 20.
Gavia Andersoni, Bruch, Cab. Journ. Orn. 1853, p. 102.
Bruchigavia Jamesoni, Pr. B. Consp. Av. ii. p. 228.
Gelastes Jamesoni, Pr. B. Compt. Rend. 1856, p. 771.
New Caledonia ; Isle of Pines.

STERNA (SYLOCHELIDON) POLIOCERCA.   B.M.
Sterna poliocerca, Gould, Proc. Z. S. 1837, p. 26 ; Cass. U. S.
Expl. Exped. 1858, p. 384.
Sterna rectirostris, Peale, U. S. Expl. Exped. p. 281.
Sylochelidon poliocerca, G. R. Gray, List of Gall. &c. B.M. p. 175.
Thalasseus poliocercus, Gould, B. of Austr. vii. pl. 24.
Feejee Islands ; Sandwich Islands?

STERNA (SYLOCHELIDON) —— ?
Sterna, n. sp., Forst. Descr. &c. p. 247.
Sterna Torresii, Gould ?
Society Islands (Oriadea).

STERNA GRACILIS.
Sterna gracilis, Gould, B. of Austr. vii. pl. 27.
New Caledonia ; Low or Paumotu Islands ; Tonga Islands.

STERNA AUSTRALIS.
Southern Tern, Lath. Gen. Syn. iii. p. 365.
Sterna australis, Gmel. S. N. i. p. 608.
Sterna media, Forst. Descr. &c. p. 20 ?
Sternula australis, Pr. B. Compt. Rend. 1856, p. 773.
Christmas Island.

STERNA VITTATA.
Wreathed Tern, Lath. Gen. Syn. iii. p. 359.
Sterna vittata, Gmel. S. N. i. p. 609.
Christmas Island.

STERNA MELANORHYNCHA.   B.M.
Sterna melanorhyncha, Gould, B. of Austr. vii. pl. 26.
Sterna velox, Gould.
Feejee Islands.

STERNA LUNATA.

Sterna lunata, Peale, U. S. Expl. Exped. p. 382.

Low or Paumotu Islands (Vincennes Island).

STERNA (STERNULA) MELANAUCHEN (?).

Sterna melanauchen, Temm. Pl. Col. 427 ; Gould, B. of Austr. vii. pl. 28.

Loyalty Islands ; New Caledonia.

STERNA (ONYCHOPRION) SERRATA.

Sterna fuliginosa, Gmel. S. N. i. p. 605 ?
Haliplana serrata, Pr. B. Compt. Rend. 1856, p. 772.
Haliplana fuliginosa, Wagl. Isis, 1832, p. 1224.
Onychoprion fuliginosus ?, Gonld, B. of Austr. vii. pl. 32.
Sterna serrata, Forst. Descr. &c. p. 276; G. Forst. Icon. ined. 110.
Onychoprion serrata, Wagl. Isis, 1832, p. 277.
Sterna guttata, Forst. Descr. &c. p. 211.
Sterna oahuensis, Bloxh. Byron's Voy. p. 251.
Haliphana panayensis, pt., Pr. B. Compt. Rend. 1856, p. 772.
Ellis's Icon. ined. 55.
'Taa' of the natives of the Marquesas Islands.

New Caledonia; Low or Paumotu Islands ; Sandwich Islands ; Cook's Islands ; Turtle and Christmas Islands ; Marquesas Islands.

GYGIS CANDIDA.   B.M.

White Tern, Lath. Gen. Syn. iii. p. 363.
Sterna candida, Forst. Descr. &c. p. 179 ; Gmel. S. N. i. p. 607;
Mus. Carls. t. 11 ; Ellis's Icon. ined. 56 ; Banks's Icon. ined. 33.
Sterna alba, Lath. Ind. Orn. ii. p. 808.
Gygis candida, Wagl. ; Gould, B. of Austr. vii. pl. 30.
'Tera-pòpa' or 'Itaé' of the natives of the Society Islands.
'Epeirai' or 'Piraë' of the natives of Otaheite.

Tonga Islands (Eaoowe or Eooa, Tongatabu) ; Feejee, Samoan, and Low Islands ; Marquesas Islands (St. Christina or Waitahoo) ; Society Islands (Otaheite, Huaheine, Borabora or Bolabola) ; Coral, Christmas, and Turtle Islands ; Caroline Islands ; Gilbert's Islands.

Note.—The late Prince Bonaparte gives three species in Compt. Rend. 1856, p. 773 : viz. *Gygis alba,* Sparrm. ; *G. candida,* Forst. ; and *G. Napoleonis,* Pr. B. ; but I have not met with any characters by which he distinguishes them from one another.

ANOÜS STOLIDUS.

Sterna stolida, Linn. S. N. i. p. 227 ; Kittl. Kupf. Vög. t. 34. f. 1.
Anoüs niger, Steph. Gen. Zool. xiii. p. 140.
Anoüs stolidus, G. R. Gray, List of Gen. of B. 1841, p. 100 ;
Gould, B. of Austr. vii. pl. 34.
Megalopterus stolidus, Peale.
'Oiyo' of the natives of the Society Islands.
Society Islands (Otaheite) ; Sandwich Islands ; Low or Paumotu

Islands; Caroline Islands; Gilbert's Islands (Kingsmill Group); Marquesas Islands; Tonga Islands; New Caledonia; Cook's Islands (Otakootaia); and coral reefs of the South Sea.

ANOÜS LEUCOCAPILLUS.

Anoüs leucocapillus, Gould, B. of Austr. vii. pl. 36 ; Cass. U. S. Expl. Exped. 1858, p. 392.
Sterna tenuirostris, (Temm.) Peale, U. S. Expl. Exped. p. 284.
Low or Paumotu Islands.

ANOÜS PARVULUS.

Anoüs parvulus, Gould, Proc. Z. S. 1845, p. 104 ; Cass. U. S. Expl. Exped. 1858, p. 393.
Megalopterus plumbeus, Peale, U. S. Expl. Exped. p. 285.
Procelsterna cinerea, pt., Pr. B. Compt. Rend. 1856, p. 773.
Christmas Island ; Low or Paumotu Islands (Honden Island).

PELECANIDÆ.

PHAËTON ÆTHEREUS.

Phaëton æthereus, Linn. S. N. i. p. 219.
Phaëton Catesbaei, Brandt.
Phaëton melanorhynchos, Gmel. S. N. i. p. 582?
‘ Haingo ’ of the natives of the Society Islands.
‘ Toolaise ’ of the natives of the Friendly Islands.

Sandwich Islands; Low or Paumotu Islands (Bow Island); Society Islands (Otaheite) ; Friendly Islands ; New Caledonia ; Caroline Islands ; Palmerston and Christmas Islands.

PHAËTON CANDIDUS.

Pelecanus aethereus, var. β, Gmel. S. N. i. p. 582.
Phaëton candidus, G. R. Gray, Gen. of B. iii. p. 663.
Phaëton flavirostris, Brandt.
G. R. Gray & Mitch. Gen. of B. pl. 183.
‘ Toake ’ of the natives.
Marquesas Islands.

PHAËTON (PHŒNICURUS) RUBRICAUDA.

Phaëton rubricauda, Bodd. Tabl. Pl. Enl. p. 57.
Phaëton phoenicuros, Gmel. S. N. i. p. 583 ; Gould, B. of Austr. vii. pl. 73.
Banks's Icon. ined. 31 ; Ellis's Icon. ined. 48.
‘ Twagge ’ of the natives of the Society Islands.
‘ Totto ’ of the natives of the Friendly Islands.

Palmerston and Turtle Islands; Cook's Islands (Harvey Island) ; Samoan or Navigators' Islands; Low or Paumotu Islands ; Society Islands (Otaheite) ; Friendly Islands ; Tonga Islands (Pylstaarts or La Sola Island).

SULA PERSONATA.

Sula personata, Gould, B. of Austr. vii. pl. 77.
Sula piscator, (L.) Peale, U. S. Expl. Exped. p. 273.
Sula cyanops, Sundev. Isis, 1842, p. 858.
Forst. Icon. ined. 107 ; Banks's Icon. ined. 30.
Low or Paumotu Islands (Honden Island).

SULA FIBER.

Pelecanus plotus, Forst. Descr. &c. p. 278 ; G. Forst. Icon. ined.
108.
Pelecanus fiber, Linn. S. N. i. p. 218.
Pelecanus sula, Linn. S. N. i. p. 218 ; Forst. Descr. &c. p. 211.
Sula fusca, (Briss.) Gould, B. of Austr. vii. pl. 78.
Sula fiber, G. R. Gray, List of Gall. &c. B.M. p. 183.

New Caledonia ; Gilbert's Islands (Kingsmill Group) ; Low or
Paumotu Islands ; Society Islands (Huaheine, Oriadea) ; Marquesas
Islands ; Palmerston and Christmas Islands ; Samoan or Navigators'
Islands (Rose or Rosa Island).

SULA (PISCATRIX) PISCATOR.

Pelecanus piscator, Linn. S. N. i. p. 217.
Pelecanus bassana, Forst. Descr. &c. p. 211 ?
Sula piscator, Gould, B. of Austr. vii. pl. 79.
Sula erythrorhyncha, Less. Tr. d'Orn. p. 601.
Sula rubripes, Gould, Proc. Z. S. 1837, p. 156.
Sula rubripeda, Peale, U. S. Expl. Exped. p. 274.
' Tococvo ' of the natives of the Marquesas Islands.

Low or Paumotu Islands (Honden Island) ; Marquesas Islands ;
Society Islands (Huaheine, Oriadea) ; Tonga Islands ?

ATAGEN AQUILUS.

Pelecanus Aquilus, Linn. S. N. i. p. 216.
Tachypetes Aquilus, Illiger.
Fregata aquila, Cuv.
Pelecanus Palmerstoni, Gmel. S. N. i. p. 573 ?
Tachypetes Palmerstoni, Cass. U. S. Expl. Exped. 1858, p. 359 ?
Pelecanus leucocephalus, Gmel. S. N. i. p. 572.
Pelecanus minor, Lath. Ind. Orn. p. 885 ; Less. Tr. p. 607.
Atagen aquilus, G. R. Gray, Gen. of B. iii. p. 669.
Edw. Birds, pl. 309.

Sandwich Islands ; Low or Paumotu Islands (Honden, Bow, and
Ducie's Islands) ; Ladrone or Marian Islands ; New Caledonia ; Marquesas Islands ; Palmerston and Christmas Islands ; Samoan or Navigators' Islands (Rose or Rosa Island).

ADDENDA.

Page 1.—*Add* to CUNCUMA LEUCOGASTER :
Falco oceanica, Less. Voy. de la Coqu. Zool. i. p. 343 ; Temm.
Pl. Col. 49.
Friendly Islands.

Page 19.—*For* LUCIDA *read* LUCIDUS.

Page 23.—*Add* to EDOLIUS COMICE :
Edolius cineraceus, var. ?, Less.
' Comice ' of the natives.

Page 42.—*Place between* CARPOPHAGA PISTRINARIA and C. LA-
TRANS :

CARPOPHAGA OCHROPYGIA.
Carpophaga ochropygia, Pr. B. Consp. Av. ii. p. 33.
Feejee Islands (Balaou).

INDEX.

THE END.

PRINTED BY TAYLOR AND FRANCIS, RED LION COURT, FLEET STREET.